The Palestinian Caper

A Black Ops Thriller

Bill Burke

BeachHouse Books

Chesterfield Missouri USA

Copyright © 2013 Bill Burke

ISBN 9781596300897

Library of Congress LCCN 2014930135

www.beachhousebooks.com

BeachHouse Books

An Imprint of
Science & Humanities Press,

Chesterfield, Missouri, USA

Dedication

This tale is dedicated to my lovely wife, Anita, who was my constant and courageous companion during our travels in the Middle East, Near East, and North Africa. I would be amiss if I did not also dedicate the tale to my many business colleagues, friends, and casual acquaintances whom I associated with while working and studying in the Middle East.

~~~

Acknowledgements

To the associates in my writers' group, I thank you for your patience, encouragement, support, and invaluable critiques while I developed the manuscript for this tale. This exceptional group also supported me while developing the manuscripts for my last four books.

In addition, I acknowledge my very good friend, Leo, for his review and superb critique of my manuscript. Leo's military intelligence expertise, and astute knowledge of spy agencies due to his liaison experience with foreign and domestic intelligence agencies, were extremely useful during his review and certainly added credibility to my novel.

A final acknowledgement goes to another dear friend, Richard, for his acute review of the manuscript. As an avid reader of spy novels, Richard's suggestions were especially helpful during the polishing phase of my manuscript development.

Preface

The constant danger of hostilities in the region was very apparent when my wife and I crossed the Jordan River on the Allenby Bridge, in a rickety old bus, from Jordan to the West Bank territory of Palestine. Heavy machineguns faced each other across the Biblical waterway, and we underwent extensive body searches at the Israeli Customs House.

During our shared taxi ride from the frontier to Jerusalem, Israel, the other two passengers questioned my wife and me incessantly during the entire trip. They were well dressed and looked like ordinary businessmen. However, they asked where we were from, where we currently lived, where we had been recently, and why we were in Israel … all in great detail. I surmised they were Shin Bet agents, the Israeli Internal Intelligence Agency, and were suspicious of us because we were living and working in Tehran, Iran … a Muslim majority nation. We also had visa stamps in our passports from Morocco, Egypt, and Jordan … all Arab Muslim nations, plus Turkey, another Muslim nation.

My treks in the State of Israel took me from Jerusalem in the east to Jaffa in the west. I also traveled to the Lebanon border in the north, and from the Syrian frontier in the east to Acre in the west within the northern part of Israel. At the Jordan River outlet of the Sea of Galilee, my wife and I touched the water together while holding hands, which tradition claims will make a marriage last for eternity. We also stayed overnight at Kibbutz Lavi overlooking the beautiful Sea of Galilee, and the Horns of Hattin Plain where Saladin defeated the Crusaders in 1187 and subsequently recaptured Jerusalem. At Lavi, we drank tea in the home of a kibbutznik family. During our enjoyable and educational conversation, we were cautioned about picking up buttons and pens on the sidewalks in the cities, because the Palestinian Liberation Organization bobby-trapped them with explosives meant to blow off little fingers and hands of Israeli children.

While visiting The Good Fence border crossing from Lebanon at Metullal, .50-caliber Israeli machineguns faced Lebanon across the narrow strip of no-man's-land. Moreover, I was able to go into one the many sandbag-lined machinegun nests and talk to the Israeli Defense Force troops. While at the border, I also talked to Lebanese Christians crossing the frontier into Israel to work, which is why it was called "The Good Fence". In broken English, combined with a little French, they were able to tell me how difficult and stressful their life was in Lebanon. We then proceeded on to the Hula Valley, the Gilan Mountains, and along the Mediterranean coastline to Tel Aviv.

Old Jerusalem was certainly a highlight of my travels. Walking in the footsteps of Jesus along the Via Dolorosa and praying at the Stations of the Cross all the way to Mount Calvary was an unsurpassed religious experience for me. We arrived at Jaffa Gate one day just minutes after a PLO terrorist bomb blew up a Jewish tourist shop on David Street. It's lucky we merely meandered from our hotel that day. My wife and I also had the pleasure of dancing the *hora*, a popular Israeli folk dance, in New Jerusalem.

My travels in the West Bank territory took me from Hebron in the south to Jenin in the north, and from Jericho and the Dead Sea in the east to Old Jerusalem in the west. This is nearly the length and essentially the breadth of the territory. Of course, like multitudes of other Christian pilgrims over the millenniums, we visited many Biblical sites along the way. On these West Bank excursions, I firmly believed the Israeli tour bus drivers had Uzi submachine guns in satchels on the floor next to them because we were in a war zone.

I also traveled the length of the Golan Heights region of Syria. This was prior to the unilateral annexation of the area by Israel in 1981, and during this excursion, the Golan Heights was under Israeli Military Administration. We traversed Jacob's Ford Bridge crossing on the Jordan River, and visited the Golani Brigade Monument and Museum. These modernistic but somber structures were erected in memory of the brave Israeli IDF soldiers who died there during the 1973 Yom Kippur War. Signs cautioning visitors about hidden land mines near the walkway certainly gave me an imminent sense of danger, perhaps because I was trained to locate such mines during my Korean War era tour of duty in the U.S. Army.

From there, we went on to El Quenitera, past the United Nations barracks in the demilitarized buffer zone, through several Druze villages, and on to the southern slopes of Biblical Mount Hermon. While at Baniyas, one of the sources of the Jordan River, PLO artillery shells heading for Israeli villages whistled overhead. Of course, my wife and I instinctively ducked down as the sounds of the artillery fire reached us and echoed in the canyons.

However, I must add, I did *not* visit Cyprus or the Gaza Strip .

During these treks, I talked to the local residents, sampled their ethnic cuisines, and observed their customs and nuances. Therefore, I attempted to give the reader a feeling of actually being in those locations by briefly introducing the language, dress, food, aromas, terrain, and sights of the region. The locations in my tale *are* real places.

This is a work of fiction and does not depict actual

incidents, except for current headline news and historical events. It is also a sequel to my novel, *The Persian Caper*, which was published in 2011. Four of the main characters from the previous book appear in this story.

Of course, all of the characters are fabricated and any names of actual people, living or dead, are purely coincidental. I selected many of them from ethnic name lists available on the Internet. Nevertheless, the characters are realistic, with all-too-human foibles and emotions. An occasional touch of irony and humor enhanced my character development.

Some foreign words and phrases appear in my book. I did this to give the reader an impression of the local populaces and the characters in my story. However, the Middle Eastern words are spelled phonetically. The reader may refer to the Glossary section in the Appendix for definitions of foreign terms, acronyms, and state-of-the-art military equipment used in this tale.

Readers may note that I used American and European automobiles in my tale. This is essentially because cars from the States and Europe were very popular in the Middle East when I lived, worked, studied, and traveled in the region. However, Asian vehicles may also be popular in the Middle East today.

In the Appendix, the descriptions of my main protagonists who are the heroes and heroines, as well as their antagonists who are the villains, can be found in the Principal Characters section. The maps are my hand-drawn artist's conceptions and are certainly not to scale, but they do provide approximate locations for a general idea of where my tale takes place.

A final note: Some readers may question the ability of my heroes to make some of the unbelievable accurate shots I described in the tale. Let me assure you that I personally have made many of those shots while shooting several of the pistols mentioned in my tale, as well as Uzi, MAC-10, HK MP5, and HK UMP40 submachine guns during my many training exercises on the range. Moreover, the Uzi *is* my favorite weapon.

Please be assured, I am not advocating attacks on the Palestinians, any political or religious groups, or the Arab nations surrounding Israel. Remember, this is a work of fiction! So, please just sit back, relax, and enjoy this intriguing, exciting, yet true-to-life novel about a capricious spy escapade. I sincerely hope it will be a vicarious experience for you!

Bill Burke

All that is necessary for the triumph of evil is for good men to do nothing.

Edmund Burke

~~~

Contents

Prologue 1

Chapter One: Cyprus 3

Larnaka 3

Paphos 9

Larnaka 16

Chapter Two: Israel 17

Tel Aviv 17

Kibbutz Lavi 19

Tel Aviv 22

Old Jerusalem 31

Tel Aviv 36

Chapter Three: West Bank 39

Tel Aviv 39

Ramallah 40

Nablus 43

Tubas 47

Jericho 56

Bethlehem 59

Hebron 61

Tel Aviv 66

Chapter Four: Gaza Strip 69

Tel Aviv 70

Al Qubban 75

Beit Hanun 78

Gaza City 82

Deir Al-Balah 89

Khan Yunis..90

Rafah 94

Chapter Five: Israel..102

Tel Aviv 102

Nazareth 103

Kibbutz Lavi...105

Sea Of Galilee..107

Golan Heights..108

Metulla...110

Haifa...111

Mount Carmel...112

Appendix...119

List Of Characters..120

Protagonists..120

Antagonists 122

Other Characters 122

Weapons List..124

Pistols 124

Assualt Rifles..124

Machine Guns 125

Rocket Propelled Grenade Launchers.......................125

Rockets 125

Drones 125

Bombs..125

Glossary 126

Fanatics have their dreams, wherewith they weave a paradise for a sect.

John Keats

~~~

THE PALESTINIAN CAPER

BY BILL BURKE

THE PALESTINIAN CAPER

Prologue

American CIA Agent Patrick O'Leary and Israeli Mossad Agent Zivah Benjamin, along with three other multi-national covert operatives, successfully observed and documented important nuclear research and development sites in Iran. They subsequently transmitted the data collected to CIA Headquarters, where experts evolved a plan to stop Iran's nuclear weapon development. Upon completion of The Persian Caper mission, Pat discovered that Zivah had asked her immediate supervisor, Chief Ariel Mazar, if he could be assigned to Mossad as a liaison officer in Tel Aviv. Just then, an Iranian agent blew up the team's vehicle parked right below Pat and Zivah's Ankara hotel room balcony.

Both of their supervisors agreed to Zivah's request, and Pat was transferred to Israel as the CIA's Chief Middle East Liaison Agent. With the mission behind them, Pat and Zivah took an early Aegean Airlines flight out of Ataturk International Airport near Istanbul, in the Republic of Turkey. The infatuated couple was heading to Cyprus for a much-needed rest and recuperation holiday.

The jetliner flew southwest, the length of the dark Sea of Marmara and above the western tip of Asian Turkey just south of the Dardanelles Strait. They then flew across the deep blue Aegean Sea and over the island of Khalkis, where Athenians drove the Persian army into the sea with an infantry charge about 500 years before Christ was born.

After a short delay at Athens, in the Hellenic Republic of Greece, the couple boarded another Aegean Airlines jetliner and headed toward Larnaka, Cyprus. The jetliner flew southeast across the Aegean Sea and above the Cyclides

1

island group near the island of Patmos, where the Apostle John wrote the *Book of Revelation* while in exile. The plane passed over Rhodes, which had a sparkling ring of green sea surrounding the island, and then above the blue-hued eastern Mediterranean Sea. They flew near towering 6,406-foot Mount Olympus in southwestern Cyprus and landed at Larnaka International Airport on the outskirts of Larnaka, in the Greek sector of the Republic of Cyprus. The 940-mile journey from Istanbul took about three hours.

Chapter One: Cyprus

Larnaka

Pat and Zivah had checked into the five-star Golden Bay Hotel on Larnaka Bay after flying in from Turkey. They freshened up, and then walked along Palm Beach Avenue on their way to the Kudeta restaurant, a well-known dining spot. "Patrick, my sixth sense tells me we're being watched."

He nodded toward a group of sailors and surmised, "It's probably all those young, handsome Greek seamen admiring a splendid specimen of Middle Eastern womanhood as you walked by them! I imagine they fell in love with your beautiful jet-black hair and lovely olive complexion, as well as your alluring body."

Smiling sweetly, Zivah responded, "Maybe it's all those young, sexy-looking Cypriot females we just walked past. They seemed to be admiring your sexy Adonis-like features, six-foot stature, and curly black hair, and Spanish-Irish complexion, Dear. They probably think you're from the region because of your slightly dark skin tone. Although, you are much taller than the locals."

"Who knows?" Pat grinned, took a deep breath, and then said, "But, in our profession we need to be suspicious and alert." A few minutes later, he added, "Zivah, the tempting aromas from all these seafood restaurants are making me hungry."

"Me too. I really enjoy strolling along this picturesque seafront district, but let's pick up the pace a little."

"Okay. Let's go!"

3

~~~

The sensual forty-year-old's seductive dark brown eyes were piercing, and her smooth-skinned face was solemn as she leaned toward Patrick and whispered, "Don't look now, but a handsome, dark-complexioned man with blondish hair is watching us intently from the bar area in back of you. He's wearing a white dinner jacket and a black bowtie. I'll get up and go toward the powder room, and then look back at you just as I walk past him."

Aware of a potential threat and in a red alert state now, Pat cautioned, "Be careful, Zivah. He may be a friendly, or he may be an enemy. I'll text you when you get to the powder room."

Pat's .380 Walther PPK was easy to reach and ready for action in his shoulder holster. He had learned early in his twenty years as a covert field agent to have his weapon accessible and ready for combat at all times, and this practice had saved his life on several occasions. Although merely out on the town with his lover on their first day in Cyprus, tonight was no exception to his cardinal rule.

Pat stood up when Zivah arose, and then watched the diminutive beauty walk gracefully toward the bar. Her lightweight blue and white print summer dress swished from the movement of her hips, and Pat murmured, "What a woman!" He made eye contact with the man in the white dinner jacket, who quickly turned away and continued watching the attractive woman and her absolutely perfect hourglass figure in the bar mirror. *Maybe he's just admiring Zivah's beautiful body,* Pat contemplated.

As she walked past the man, Zivah glanced back at Pat and nodded slightly. He then sent a text message to her with his BlackBerry, *can't identify him. not irani. see if he follows when we leave. use utmost caution.*

While occasionally glancing toward the man at the bar, Pat and Zivah enjoyed each other's company over a glass of local Lambouri red wine at the popular restaurant in the Makenzy district near Larnaka Castle. "Patrick, that Cypriot meal was simply scrumptious, especially the *koupepias.* I've always loved stuffed grape leaves, but they were exceptional tonight."

"I agree, they were delightful. As you may know, they are called *dolmades* in Greece," Pat responded. "I also savored the spicy *pastourma.*"

"Yes, that dish was good too. But, I bet you weren't aware that *pastourma* was made with camel meat instead of beef many years ago. I wouldn't have eaten it if they made it that way today!"

After the playful bantering, Pat thought a moment, then smiled as he asked, "Well, what do you think of Aphrodite's island so far?"

"Ah, the Greek goddess of love and sensual beauty! This is an appealing island, and I would like to explore it ... at least the Greek sector. I've had enough of Turks for a while, so I'll pass on seeing the Turkish sector on the north side of the island. Perhaps I'll learn some of Aphrodite's love-making secrets if we just travel to Paphos!"

"Great, I'm all for that! Not that you need to learn more about love-making, Zivah." Then he grinned and playfully expressed, "You probably know that the ancient Romans called her Venus."

She nodded, smiled back, and replied, "Yes, I did know that."

"I understand the Turks call their side of the island the Turkish Republic of Cyprus, but it's not recognized by the United Nations or any country except Turkey."

"That's right, Patrick. It's an illegal entity."

"By the way, I vividly remember what you said in Ankara last week, and I quote, 'Maybe we can find a golden sand beach in a secluded cove and go skinny-dipping in the warm Mediterranean, just as the Greek goddess of love and beauty did.'"

Zivah beamed, and responded, "I did say that ... and I meant it!"

They finished their wine and Pat paid the waiter. Then he uttered softly, "I just thought of something. I may have seen Mister White Dinner Jacket sitting in our hotel lobby earlier. Act casual when we leave, and don't look at him. But, be prepared for a possible assault when we're outside the restaurant."

She nodded knowingly and patted the 9-millimeter Sig Sauer Sub-Compact in her evening purse, "I'm ready for anything, Patrick."

They walked out onto the sidewalk and Pat whispered in Zivah's ear, "Hail that cab coming down the street. Meanwhile, I'll step into the shadows and wait for him to come out."

Zivah waved down the taxi and opened the rear door when it came to a complete stop. Just then, Mister White Dinner Jacket emerged from the restaurant and looked puzzled when he saw Zivah getting into the taxi alone. However, it was too late. Pat jumped out of the shadows from behind him and had a stranglehold on the man's neck with his forearm before he could react. Pat ordered, "Tell me who you are and why you are watching us, or I'll break your scrawny neck."

"I'm CIS Agent Christo Alexander. My identification is in my vest pocket, Agent O'Leary. I'll take it out, with your permission, and I will not resist."

Pat kept a stranglehold on the man as he looked at his photo ID. He then released him and said, "Okay, Agent Alexander. The CIA has always worked closely with the Greek National Intelligence Service and the Cyprus Intelligence Service. So, what's this all about?"

Meanwhile, Zivah had exited the taxi and was standing by Pat with a grip on her Sig Sauer.

"Greek NIS sent us intel about an Iranian Takavar commando, Major Mohammad Amir, who is looking for you and Agent Benjamin because of deadly incidents you were involved with in Tehran and Isfahan last week." He nodded at Zivah and continued, "We knew you two were in Cyprus as soon as you went through Passport Control at the airport. So, I was observing you in case Amir showed up here in Cyprus. Look ... I have his picture on my cell phone."

Zivah released her grip on the SIG. Then she and Pat carefully peered at the image. Pat exclaimed, "That looks like the *Irani* that blew up the OHD limo in front of the Ankara Hilton when we were smooching on our balcony right above it!"

"Yes that's him," Zivah agreed.

"He's after me because I took out several Iranian VEVAK agents, as well as a well-known Russian SVR agent in Tehran during my last mission," Pat explained.

Zivah added, "And I took out several Iranian Revolutionary Guardsmen and a major VEVAK field agent near Isfahan during that same mission."

"Yes, we know all about the demise of Andrei Desnov and Doctor Ali Kermani. Favorable news travels fast in our business, and I say, 'good riddance!'"

"What's our next move, Agent Alexander?" Pat asked.

"We wait until Amir catches up with you. So, just act normal and do whatever you had made plans to do during your holiday. If and when he appears, CIS will take it from there and that Iranian will disappear. I promise you on the graves of my namesakes, Christ and Alexander the Great."

"You do know that Takavar commandos seldom work alone?"

"Agent O'Leary, we're prepared for that. I'm also not alone." Just then, a lithe, attractive female Cypriot with pretty auburn hair and luminous blue eyes walked up to the group. "Agents O'Leary and Benjamin, meet my backup, CIS Agent Halie Georgandas."

The two striking women nodded and shook hands as they eyed each other from head to toe. *Stay away from my Patrick*, Zivah mulled.

With a wide grin and an approving look, Pat greeted the attractive woman with "My pleasure, Agent Georgandas." He paused a few seconds, then continued, "Agent Benjamin sensed someone watching us as we walked along Palm Beach Avenue this evening. Was that the two of you?"

Christo nodded. "Yes, I mingled with a group of Greek sailors as you walked by."

"And I was chatting with a group of young Cypriot girls," Halie added.

"Wait a minute! I'm on R and R holiday and I don't like being the bait. I would feel like a lamb waiting for a Persian leopard to attack!" Zivah exclaimed as she scanned the street looking for Amir.

To soothe her, Pat replied, "I'll be by your side constantly, and we can watch out for each other," as he smiled and winked at her.

She smiled back, shrugged her shoulders, and said softly, "I'm ready now, Patrick. But, stay away from *her!*" as she tipped her head toward Halie.

"Agent Alexander, we agree with the plan. Let's exchange cell phone numbers," Pat suggested. "Zivah and I will notify our respective chiefs of the situation."

After texting Ariel Mazar, Zivah received an immediate reply, *watch your backs!*

Paphos

While dining on a Cyprus-style breakfast buffet at the hotel's Yacht Club Restaurant, Pat and Zivah watched the sun rise over the glittering Mediterranean Sea. "Patrick, this is gorgeous! Look at all the beautiful colors dancing on the water!"

"Yes. Not only do we have a fantastic sunrise, but we also have a great view of Larnaka Bay. I'm admiring all those sleek, multi-million dollar yachts in the harbor. What a life!"

"Maybe some day we can do some yachting." After a short pause, Zivah continued, "I certainly enjoyed the breakfast *glykos*. They were delicious!"

"And, I loved the flavor of the *flaounes* pastries. They were a perfect match for the extra-strong Greek coffee." Pat looked pensive for a moment, "Zivah, let's rent a car today and drive down the coast to Paphos, the legendary birthplace of Aphrodite."

"I'm all for that, Dear. So long as Major Mohammad

Amir doesn't chase us down the highway!"

"Let's not worry about Amir. Christo is capable of taking care of him and his goons."

After breakfast, the two operatives rented a silver Jaguar XK sports car at Europcar Rentals on Georgiou Mouski Avenue. They drove by the ruins of ancient Kitium, and then past the marble bust of Zeno while heading west out of town. Pat suddenly exclaimed, "Look over there," as he pointed to the Church of Lazarus. "That's where Saint Lazarus, the brother of Mary and Martha, died and was buried."

"The man that Jesus raised from the dead in *The New Testament?*"

"He's the one."

The highway headed inland to the southwest and bypassed rugged Cape Kiti. Scanning the GPS map, Zivah explained, "We're nearing Khirokitia, the site of a 6,000-year-old Neolithic settlement."

"Wow! That was thousands of years before Abraham was born, and ..." Pat's words trailed off as he looked in the rearview mirror. "Hold on, we've got company."

Zivah spun around in her seat and spotted a black Mercedes-Benz sedan bearing down on them at a very high speed. "Oh, no. It must be Mohammad Amir!"

"Yep!" Pat yelled as he floor-boarded the Jaguar. "Call Christo. Tell him where we are and what's going on."

The Jaguar was traveling 160 miles per hour and the Mercedes was not able to close in on the quarter-mile gap between the vehicles. As Zivah pressed the BlackBerry speed dialer for Christo's number, she yelled, "Patrick, they're shooting at us with automatic weapons! I can see the bullets hitting the pavement behind us."

"Now, that's idiotic! They won't be able to hit us from over 1,300 yards away while on the move. We're outgunned, or I would stop and shoot it out with them."

"Christo! Christo! We're westbound on the Larnaka-Paphos Highway and a black Mercedes is pursuing us at 160 miles an hour. They're shooting at us! We just passed the Khirokitia turnoff and we're approaching Amathus."

Halie responded, "We followed the black Mercedes out of town and we're right behind them, Agent Benjamin. It's Major Amir, but they're going too fast for us to catch up to them. We'll call ahead and have a roadblock set up at Limassol."

"Watch out for a sharp curve to the right when you see the coastline. One-sixty is much too fast for that curve. You will spin out and might go over the cliff," Christo yelled into the speaker.

Listening on Zivah's cell phone speaker, Pat replied, "I can handle the curve. You just handle Amir." He downshifted just before entering the dangerous curve, let the engine's compression slow them down a little, then floor-boarded the vehicle as he entered the curve. The Jaguar hugged the road and pulled out of the curve like an Indy 500 racecar. "Wow! I sure love this Jag!" Pat exclaimed with a big grin.

Zivah giggled nervously. "And, I just love the driver!" She looked over her shoulder and announced with glee, "They spun out on the curve!"

Pat chuckled. "Maybe they'll wind up in the sea!" He then slowed down as they entered the town of Amathus.

"Patrick, they're still in pursuit and getting closer!" yelled Zivah.

"Not for long!" Pat geared down going through the town

11

and blared the horn to warn locals they were traveling through very fast. At the far end of town, he hollered, "Hold on!" as the Jaguar shot forward and reached 160 in a few seconds.

The Mercedes was now just barely keeping pace with the Jaguar on a long straightaway. Zivah cautioned, "They're less than a quarter of a mile behind now, and they're shooting at us again!"

Zivah's BlackBerry rang and Halie informed them, "We almost caught up to the Iranians when they spun out on the curve, but we can't shoot at them now because they're too close to you and you're in the line of fire." She paused, then continued, "Okay, the roadblock is ready to set up. They'll let you through, then close the road behind you. Amir will not get through!"

"That's good news. We're glad you're watching our backs," Pat responded. A few minutes later, he took his foot off the accelerator pedal and geared down. The Jaguar slowed as he downshifted through three gears when they neared the Limassol roadblock. Several police cars blocked the road and shoulders and a helicopter hovered above them after they drove through. With stone walls lining both sides of the highway for several hundred yards, the trap was set.

"Well, Patrick, we're out of harm's way. Thank you, *Adonai*. My prayers were answered! My nerves are sure on edge, but I can relax now."

"Great! We'll let Christo and Halie handle Amir and his goons. Quick, look back. They have Amir's only way out of the trap blocked, and they're shooting it out."

Looking back, Zivah exclaimed, "I see! The Cypriots sure know what they're doing."

"We'll let CIS interrogate any survivors of the shootout.

It's their turf and there's no reason for us to go back." Pat continued driving at the speed limit through Limassol, the biggest port on the island. Back on the Larnaka-Paphos Highway, he picked up speed. "Now that the excitement is over, we can enjoy the spectacular coastal scenery."

"Yes, it's lovely. However, I'm still trembling from the adrenalin surges during the chase."

"You'll calm down in a few minutes. Just take a few deep breaths once in awhile, and enjoy the mild, subtropical Mediterranean climate."

"I will. The weather's just like the seashore back home."

Following the rugged coastline, the two operatives went past steep cliffs and black, rock-strewn beaches. After passing through the quaint seacoast village of Epsikopi, Pat asked, "Okay, Zivah. Where are the golden sand beaches?"

Calmed down and finally over her trembling, she replied, "I don't know. But, if Aphrodite could find them, so can we!"

A few minutes later, they drove into Paphos. "Here we are ... the mythical birthplace of the love goddess. Look over there. Those huge foundation walls must be the remnants of the vast Temple of Aphrodite."

"Yes, and I can certainly see why she chose this beautiful island for her playground. Patrick, I need a drink after that stimulating chase. Perhaps a tall tropical cocktail."

"Me too. I'm accustomed to being the chaser, not the chasee."

Zivah answered her cell phone, and Christo excitedly expressed, "We took out Major Mohammad Amir and the four commandos in his team during a firefight. There's no survivors, and your problems are over for now. No need for you to return, so enjoy the rest of your holiday."

Pat replied, "Thanks, Christo. However, our problems with the Iranians may not be over yet."

"That's right," Zivah chimed in.

"I know what you mean. But, Tehran will not find out about the incident until you're out of my country tomorrow," replied Christo. "Of course, you know better than I do, Iran supports Hamas in the Gaza Strip and Hezbollah in Lebanon, so watch yourselves if you go near those territories. Take care of each other, and until we meet again, God be with you!"

"And also with you, my friend. *Ciao!*" Pat responded.

"*Adonai* be by your side, Christo and Halie," Zivah added.

Pat and Zivah phoned their chiefs and gave them an update. Then they traveled through the ancient Roman capital of Cyprus while looking for an inviting tavern. "Did you know, Zivah, that Paphos is where the Apostle Paul struck a sorcerer blind?"

"No, I didn't. I don't know very much about *The New Testament*. You'll have to read it with me some day."

"I will. The story is in the book of *Acts*. Hey, that little *taverna* looks quiet and not too busy."

"Oh, I see it, the Apomero. It's right on the harbor and it looks quaint and romantic. Let's stop there, Patrick."

While the two operatives enjoyed their refreshing rum cocktails on a veranda overlooking the harbor, Pat questioned the proprietor, "This is the third largest island in the Mediterranean Sea, so there must be a nice, secluded golden sand beach somewhere. Perhaps even a nudist beach. Can you help us find what we are looking for?"

"Mister, you will not find nudist beaches in Cyprus!

Cypriots are much too conservative for that." He thought a moment, ogled Zivah and visualized her being naked, then smiled and added, "However, we look the other way when airline hostesses and tourists are bare-topped or completely nude at Agios Georgios Beach. It is located in a cove just north of Paphos."

"How do we find this beach?" Zivah inquired with a wide grin.

~~~

Agios Georgios was a sun-kissed golden sand beach in a secluded cove. "Now, this is what I had in mind, Patrick. Just don't pay too much attention to those lovely women with their oil-covered bare breasts glistening in the sunlight!"

"I'll look, but not touch," Pat playfully replied. "Let's go down to the water's edge to disrobe and take a dip in the sea."

While body surfing naked in the swells of the warm Mediterranean, Zivah squealed, "This is fun and very sensual. I feel like Aphrodite must have felt when she swam nude in the sea!"

"The goddess of love and sensual beauty could not have had a body more beautiful than yours, My Love!"

"And Adonis could not have had a more perfect body than yours, Patrick!

After their dip in the sea, the two lovers basked in the warm rays of the sun as they caressed and admired each other's naked bodies.

Larnaka

That evening, Pat and Zivah dined at Les Etoiles in the Golden Bay Hotel. "Patrick, I just loved the classic haute cuisine."

"And the soothing live band music most certainly tops off our romantic last night in Cyprus."

The next morning, Pat and Zivah boarded a Cyprus Airways flight to Israel. The plane flew southerly across the deep-blue Mediterranean Sea and landed at Ben Gurion International Airport near Tel Aviv, in the State of Israel. The 200-mile trip took 55 minutes.

Mossad Agent Ari Jacobi, one of their Persian Caper comrades-in-arms, met them at the arrivals gate. "*Shalom!* Welcome to the Holy Land, Patrick." Ari smiled and shook Pat's hand. He then turned to greet Zivah, gave her a long brotherly hug, kissed her on both cheeks, and said warmly, "*Shalom!* Welcome back home, Zivah."

I believe they did have something going on in the past, Pat surmised.

With a heartfelt smile, she replied, "*Shalom!* I see you've recovered from your combat wound, Ari."

He grinned and replied, "It was just a flesh wound!"

Reflecting on the harrowing events of the previous mission, all three of the seasoned espionage agents broke out into nearly uncontrollable laughter.

Zivah squeezed Ari's hand and said softly, "We had some excitement in Cyprus, and we're anxious to tell you all about it!"

~~~

Chapter Two: Israel

Tel Aviv

While driving past a burned-out minibus on a city street, Zivah explained, "Patrick, *fedayeen* terrorists bombed and burned that tour bus a few years ago, and all twenty people on the bus, including the driver, were killed in the heinous attack. Our Prime Minister decided to leave it in place as a constant reminder to Israelis, and foreign tourists, that we live in an ongoing war zone. As you know, all of our Arab neighboring countries, and many of the Muslim Palestinians, at least the terrorists, want us dead."

Pat nodded and replied solemnly, "I understand. Many of them also want Americans dead. That's why I'm here."

After going down Embassy Row and passing by the American, British, and French embassies, Zivah and Ari dropped Pat off at the Hilton Tel Aviv Hotel between Hayarkan Boulevard and the shore of the Mediterranean Sea. "I'm going to rent a car and visit my parents at Kibbutz Lavi, Patrick," Zivah said as they hugged and kissed each other next to the limo. "I'll see you tomorrow at Mossad Headquarters."

"Okay, but I'll miss being with you tonight." He paused a second or two, then shook hands with Ari, smiled and continued, "Watch out for this handsome brown-haired guy. I sense a little competition for your affection."

"Don't worry, Dear, I'm all yours," Zivah replied"

Ari winked at them and grinned.

Pat checked in, and then took a long welcome shower.

He casually studied the panoramic view of the sea from his tenth floor balcony before going up to the hotel's King Solomon Grill and Terrace. While savoring a filet mignon and local Carmel red wine, he mused, *Dear, dear, Zivah, I most certainly wish you were here to enjoy this fine meal with me.*

As Pat strolled out of the hotel's main entrance, he asked the doorman, "Can I still get to the beach by walking down the hill by Independence Park?"

"Yes, you can sir. There is no access to the beach area from the back of the hotel. It is protected by coils of barbed wire ... because of unwanted *visitors!*"

"Visitors like the PLO and other terrorist *fedayeen?*"

The doorman nodded and replied, "That is correct, sir. Although the PLO is not a threat these days, other groups are. You should return to the hotel before dark."

"I see that not much has changed since the last time I stayed here," Pat responded. He then took a taxi to the American Embassy and checked-in with the CIA Station Chief. After returning to the hotel, he walked down to the white sand beach and enjoyed listening to the waves breaking, while watching the mesmerizing effervescence of the sea. As the sun began to set across the Mediterranean, Pat walked back up the hill to the main entrance of the hotel.

Several military vehicles pulled into the hotel courtyard at dusk, and a contingent of Israeli Defense Force youngsters, armed with full-automatic .30 caliber M2 Carbines. They took up positions on all four sides of the hotel and Pat thought, *Yep, just like the last time I was here!*

That night, he had pleasant thoughts about being with Zivah while dropping of into a deep, restful sleep.

Kibbutz Lavi

Zivah drove out of Tel Aviv in her rented canary yellow Porsche convertible. The warm afternoon sun glistened on the Mediterranean Sea as she headed north on the coast highway. The top was down, and the sea breeze blew gently through her wavy black hair while she listened to Hebrew songs on the radio. She mused, *I've always loved this scenic coastal drive, and I'm certainly happy to be back in my homeland.*

She turned inland at Hadera and spotted a uniformed female IDF soldier, with a 9-millimeter Uzi submachine gun slung over her shoulder, hitchhiking on the east side of the town. Slowing down, she thought, *We Israelis always pick up our soldiers when we see them hitchhiking.* Then she recognized the black-haired hitchhiker and hollered, "Cailin! Cailin Rinesmann! It's me, Zivah Benjamin. *Shalom!*"

"*Shalom,* my dear childhood friend." The muscular woman jumped into the Porsche and the two women kissed each other on both cheeks. "I see you're still as lithe as ever. How is Mossad treating you these days?"

"Very well, thank you. I'm happy with my job. Are you going to visit your parents?"

"Yes, I'm on leave for a few days."

"Good. I'm going to see my parents and will spend the night there. I have to be back in Tel Aviv early in the morning."

"Maybe we can dine together this evening."

Zivah nodded. "Guess what? I met someone on my last assignment that I'm in love with. He's just a few years older than me, and I'll tell you about Patrick on the way to the kibbutz."

"Yes, I would like to hear about him!"

19

"Great! I see you were promoted to captain since I last saw you."

"That I was. I've decided to make the army my career, at least until I'm too old to keep up with the youngsters being conscripted into the IDF. It seems they get younger every year."

"No, we just get older, my very dear friend."

The highway skirted the northern border of the Palestinian-held West Bank area, then entered Alufa. Zivah turned left in town and passed through Nazareth a few minutes later. Driving by the Grotto of Mary, and the churches of Saint Gabriel and Saint Joseph, she exclaimed, "Patrick is Catholic. I wish he were here to tell me more about the Virgin Mary and the boyhood home of Jesus! As *kibbutzniks*, we didn't learn very much about Christianity, although we went by their holy sites many, many times. Maybe I'll consider joining Jews for Jesus. What do you think, Cailin?"

"What I think really doesn't matter, but I certainly wouldn't do it. And, your parents would never agree to it, or to your getting romantically involved with someone outside our faith! However, it's your life and your decision." She paused, and then continued, "I love you like a sister, Zivah, and you will always be my dear friend, no matter what your decision is."

"Thank you for being so honest with me. Yes, we will always be friends." A few moments later, she expressed, "I want to tell you about my gorgeous hunk of a man now. He was in charge of my last mission, and we've been together since its completion last week. I can't stop thinking about him day and night, and he was even in my thoughts during an intense firefight in Iran last week."

"It sounds like infatuation to me. What does he look like, and what kind of personality does he have? Can you really get serious about someone outside of your religion?"

"I'm still in a quandary about the religious issue, and I'm fearful of telling my parents about Patrick ... especially Papa."

"Well, you will just have to work out that dilemma with your parents. I certainly wish you luck with that!"

"Patrick is in his late-forties, but young looking. He's a trim six feet tall, with curly black hair, seductive hazel eyes, a slightly dark complexion, and I think he looks like Adonis."

"Hmm. He may be someone that even *I* could fall for!"

The road went through Cana, where Jesus performed His first miracle. Zivah then turned left at the Lavi Hotel sign and entered the front gate of Kibbutz Lavi. *Now, I'm really home. I should have called Mama and Papa, instead of surprising them.* Gazing to the east, Zivah exclaimed for all to hear, "I just love this commanding view of the grassy Horns of Hattin Plain, the sparkling Sea of Galilee, and the tall, barren Golan Heights. This is where we grew up as *kibbutzniks!*"

Cailin shouted, "Hey everybody, the *kibbutznik* brats are back!"

Zivah parked the car and they walked past strategically placed bomb shelters located between every few homes. "Remember the many long nights we spent down in the shelters as children, with explosions and gunfire keeping us awake all night? The PLO was certainly active in those days."

"They were replaced by the new Palestinian terrorist groups, and they keep the IDF very, very busy. Although, they haven't hit Lavi recently. I thank *Adonai* for keeping our parents safe!"

21

"I certainly thank My Lord, as well." Zivah continued, "The terrorists sure kept me very busy when I was working for Shin Bet. I vividly remember the booby-trapped pens and dolls the terrorists placed on the ground to blow off fingers and hands of innocent Israeli children that picked them up!"

Cailin went up the walkway to her parent's home and yelled back at Zivah, "I'll see you at the dining hall tonight."

"Yes, see you then. Meat or dairy seating?"

Cailin just shrugged.

Zivah went up the next walkway to her parents' home. Mama greeted her at the front door, and they hugged and kissed each other.

"Zivah, my dear child. Papa is in the kitchen."

Papa walked into the living room, hugged his only daughter, and expressed, "Welcome back home, my little one. You must freshen up for dinner. Then, you can tell us all about your recent adventure. At least what you are permitted to tell us."

"I will, Papa, I will. And, I have much, much more to tell you and Mama ... after dinner."

Tel Aviv

The next day, Pat took a taxi to the Shalom Tower in the city center. Then he took another taxi to Petach Tikva Road, in case he was being followed. Finally, he entered The Institute for Intelligence and Special Tasks lobby at 0645 hours. Just past the huge "MOSSAD" mosaic embedded in the floor, he told the nice-looking Uzi armed female receptionist, "*Shalom!* I have an appointment with Ariel Mazar, the Mossad Special Operations Division chief, at 0700 hours," and handed her his CIA photo ID.

The receptionist made a phone call, then stated, "Chief Mazar is on her way down to sign you in, sir," as she handed Pat's ID back to him.

The attractive middle-aged woman appeared a few minute later. "*Shalom!* Nice to see you again, Agent O'Leary. Welcome to Mossad Headquarters, and my *Metsada* division."

"Thank you, Chief Mazar. I'm pleased to be here," Pat replied as he shook her hand. "Has Agent Benjamin arrived yet?"

"Yes, she's upstairs. But first, let's get you signed in and processed for your Mossad photo ID. Then we'll put you into the iris scanner database so you can get around inside headquarters."

~~~

When Ariel and Pat walked into the conference room, Zivah immediately approached and kissed him on both cheeks.

"Save the paramour affection until later," Ariel commented sternly.

Addressing the meeting attendees, Ariel announced, "It's my pleasure to welcome CIA Agent Patrick O'Leary to our counter-terrorism taskforce. He is his agency's Chief Middle East Liaison Agent." After a welcoming applause for Pat, Ariel continued, "Everyone, please introduce yourselves and give a very brief description of your formal education and professional background. I'll start. As all of you know, I'm Ariel Mazar, Mossad Special Operations Division Chief. I've been in this position for the last two years, and I report directly to 'The Prussian,' our Mossad Director.

"After my stint in the Israeli Defense Force, I attended

the University of Haifa, where I earned a Bachelor of Arts degree. I then went to Harvard in the States for my master and doctorate degrees. After my PhD graduation, Mossad offered me a position in the Political Action and Liaison Department, which I accepted. A few years later, I was transferred into this division with a promotion. I speak Arabic, French, German, and Spanish, and I'm now learning Farsi. At my level, my field operations are best kept secret, so I won't discuss them with you. Agent O'Leary, why don't you go next?"

Pat rose, smiled at the group, and winked at Zivah. "Good morning! You already know my name and current position, so I'll get right to my background. I earned a Bachelor of Science degree, and a Master of Science degree graduating with honors at Stanford University. That was after my tour in the United States Marine Corps. I speak and read Farsi, Arabic, Spanish, and French fluently. During my twenty years with The Firm, I successfully completed missions in just as many countries. My latest mission was in Iran, and I had the pleasure of meeting and working with Mossad agents Benjamin and Jacobi as their team leader during that successful assignment."

As Pat sat down, Ariel stated, "I must tell you now, Agent O'Leary, The Prussian almost vetoed my decision to accept you for our taskforce when he found out that *your* president gave $20.6 million dollars to Gaza Strip Hamas supporters for so called humanitarian aid. Then, he didn't agree with your government for not protecting your ambassador to Libya during the Benghazi incident. Lucky for you, and for our taskforce, I convinced him you will be a tremendous asset for us."

"Thank you for that, Chief Mazar, I certainly appreciate it," Pat responded with a sincere smile.

Zivah stood up and began her introduction. "*Shalom!* I'm Mossad Agent Zivah Benjamin. After my tour of duty in the IDF, I was recruited by Shin Bet. While working for that agency, I earned a BA degree at the Hebrew University in Jerusalem. I'm fluent in Farsi, Arabic, French, and English. I also have some knowledge of Russian, Turkish, and Spanish. As a Mossad agent, I accomplished covert missions in the Palestinian territories several times, as well as in Tunis, Syria, Lebanon, and in Iran twice."

As Zivah sat down, Ari rose and stated. "*Shalom!* I'm Mossad Agent Ari Jacobi. My specialty field is nuclear weapons, including dirty bombs and missile warheads. After my IDF service, I attended the Hebrew University and graduated with a BS degree. While there, I became fluent in Farsi, Arabic, French, English, and German. I also know some Kurdish and Russian. Mossad recruited me after graduation, and my covert work included assignments in Gaza, West Bank, Lebanon, Syria, Bosnia, and recently Iran."

"I guess I'm next. *As salam' alakoom* ... *Shalom!* My name is Fatin Izmiri, and I'm new to Mossad," the young, well-developed woman expressed as she fluttered her long eyelashes and smiled sweetly at Ari.

Ari admired the curvaceous, pretty young woman with light brown hair peeking out from under a colorful scarf that matched her dark, smooth complexion. Her penetrating coal-black eyes and ready smile captivated him, and he mulled, *What an attractive woman! I could become interested in her.*

Fatin continued, "I'm a Turkish-Arab Palestinian. I'm also an Antiochian Orthodox Christian, and I abhor the terrorist tactics that many of the Muslim Palestinian factions use against the Hebrews and Arab Christians. I speak English, French, Hebrew, and of course Arabic. After graduating from Northwestern University in Chicago with a

Bachelor of Arts degree, I was interviewed by Mossad to determine if they could use me in covert operations against terrorism. I was willing to work for the agency, and they accepted me, trained me, and ... well, this is my first day on the job."

Everyone in the room stood and applauded her.

"*Bonjour, comment ca va?* Oops! *Pardon moi!* I should speak English. I am DGSE Agent André Chevalier, Andrew in English but please call me André. My surname is Chevalier. I joined France's Directorate General for External Security after retiring from the French Foreign Legion. I too am degreed, with a Bachelor of Science from Paris-Sorbonne University. I speak English, Flemish, German, Russian, Arabic, Spanish, Vietnamese, and some Hebrew. My DGSE missions included liberating French journalists held hostage in Iraq, aiding in the arrest of the killers of French tourists in Mauritania, and more recently, covert work in Libya.

"Certainly there were many other world-wide missions during my Legion days." The foul smell of his French cigarettes permeated the room as the suave, gray-haired Frenchman saluted Ariel Mazar and sat down.

"Agent Chevalier, I'm surprised that 'The Prussian' also allowed you on our taskforce. Especially after the French President's made the public comment about our Prime Minister, 'I can't stand him. He's a liar.'"

"Chief Mazar, I'm not speaking for my president, but I apologize for that incident," André replied.

A tall woman with long blonde hair, a plain-Jane face, and a voluptuous figure then stood. "Good Day! I'm MI6 Agent Sarah Keats, and yes, I'm a descendant of that great English romantic poet, John Keats. I did a stint in the Special Air Force commandos prior to joining MI5. After two years, I became bored with that organization so I transferred to MI6, because ... that's where the action is. I obtained 'Double O' status after five years with MI6. I'm an alum of the University of Bath, graduating with a BA, summa cum laude. I'm fluent in French, German, Russian, Serbian, and Arabic. I also know a tad of Turkish.

"Including my SAF assignments, I've participated in missions to Morocco, Egypt, Syria, Turkey, Serbia, Afghanistan, and Russia. I believe I will like working with this taskforce. Moreover, I'm not being cheeky, but I'm very pleased that you have modern flush loos in Israel, instead of the non-flush squat toilets prevalent in the Middle East!"

Everyone in the room chuckled at her comment, and Ariel responded with, "Yes, we *are* the most modern nation in the region."

Pat admired the statuesque middle-aged woman and mulled, *What a well-preserved lady!*

As if she was reading Pat's mind, Zivah frowned at Sarah. *Lady, you had better stay away from my Patrick!*

"Okay, let's get down to business," Ariel Mazar declared. "Our multi-national taskforce was created by the Director to seek and destroy threats to Israel and the Western nations. The focus is on the Palestinian territories and, if necessary, in our contiguous Arab nations. We will work closely with our Shin Bel counterparts while operating in the Palestinian held areas, but you will be on your own if we insert you into the Arab countries.

"Now this is very important. The Palestinian people are *not* our enemies. However, the Palestinian terrorist groups are!

"Remember this, you are deep-cover combatants that will conduct lethal covert operations. Your targets will be *jihad* terrorists that may use Israel as a testing ground for weapons they intend to use in the western nations."

"Can we rely on IDF support while operating in the Palestinian territories?" Zivah inquired.

"That's a definite affirmative, Agent Benjamin, at least in the West Bank. *Sayert Matkal*, the Israeli General Staff Reconnaissance commandos, can also help when needed. Are there any other questions at this point?" After a short pause, Ariel continued, "We have been granted authority to utilize the U.S. Air Force's Advanced Extremely High Frequency satellite communications system with our BlackBerry satellite phones. Use text only ... do not make voice calls while on assignment. Our messages will be protected and untraceable with the AEHF. Use only our code names throughout the taskforce operations. Be sure to include me in *all* of your text transmissions."

Pat interrupted, "We used AEHF during my last mission in Iran, and I can assure everyone that it's a very secure and reliable system."

Zivah and Ari nodded in assent.

"Thanks for that assurance, Agent O'Leary."

Passing out lists to everyone, she continued, "You will work in two-person teams and use only your code names while in the field. Agent Benjamin, code name *Cobra,* and Agent O'Leary, code name *Viper,* will be in Team One with Benjamin the team leader."

Zivah smiled and winked at Pat.

Mazar continued, "Agent Jacobi, code name *Asp,* and Agent Keats, code name *Mamba,* will be in Team Two, with Jacobi the team leader. Agent Izmiri, code name *Coral,* and Agent Chevalier, code name *Sidewinder,* will be in Team Three with Izmiri the team leader. I will also be available to assist with Team Three because of Izmiri's lack of experience in the field, and because Chevalier is not native to our region. My code name is *Bushmaster*.

"Of course, we will keep your respective agencies informed of your assigned missions and your whereabouts. I will always know where you are in the field by the gps coordinates sent from your BlackBerrys.

Of course, your respective agencies expect us to keep them informed as well. Which I will certainly do."

Pat contemplated, *I wonder how informed?* Then he asked, "Will there be interaction between teams, such as backing each other up during a mission?"

"Good question, Agent O'Leary. That's an affirmative." Mazar thought a moment, and then continued, "However, all inter-team assistance will be determined by me. You will not unilaterally decide to help each other, because you may not see the entire picture of our operations. Only I can make those decisions. Remember, I'm in-charge here," the strong-willed woman declared.

Everyone in the conference room nodded in understanding.

"What about our personal sidearms? I prefer to carry my 9-millimeter Beretta PX4 Storm Subcompact," Sarah proffered.

"You may know, Mossad did away with the semi-automatic silencer-equipped .22-caliber Model 70 Beretta, which was before my time. Our standard issue today is a 9-millimeter semi-auto Beretta PX4 Storm compact equipped with a silencer. Agent Benjamin carries a 9-millimeter Sig Sauer Sub-Compact now. For this taskforce, she will change to the standard Beretta. Agents Jacobi and Izmiri already carry the standard Beretta. In your case Agent Keats, it's your choice."

"Thank you, Guv. I'll switch to the standard Beretta as well," Sarah replied.

Nodding at Pat, Mazar continued, "However, I know Agent O'Leary carries a .380-caliber Walther PPK, and he should consider changing to a standard 9-millimeter Beretta while on this taskforce. That way your pistol ammo will be compatible with our Uzis, as well as the magazines being interchangeable with other taskforce members weapons."

"I certainly will, Chief Mazar," Pat responded.

"Moreover, Agent Chevalier carries a .380-caliber Manhurin PPK/S. Are you willing to make the change to the standard Beretta, Chevalier?"

"*Mais oui*, but yes, *Madame*. I will comply, *Merci*," André replied.

"Good! Everyone will carry our standard PX4 Beretta while on a mission for this taskforce.

"One last item … leave your religious medals here while on assignment. I see that Agent O'Leary has a Saint Patrick's medal around his neck, and Agents Jacobi and Benjamin are wearing Star of David necklaces, which are admirable but will get you killed in the Palestinian Territories. Well, it's settled then. That's it for now. You have the afternoon off, but be back in this conference room at 0700 hours tomorrow. Report here at that time every day from now on, except for Saturdays, which is our *Sabbat*, and while you're on a mission. *Shalom!*"

As the taskforce members left the conference room, Zivah suggested, "Let's all go to Old Jerusalem for a meal. It's about forty miles away, and I know a great mom and pop type restaurant in the Jewish Quarter that serves the very best kosher food."

"Sounds good to me," Pat agreed.

Patting his stomach, Ari added, "Me too. I'm famished.!"

Old Jerusalem

The Mossad limousine driver took the six taskforce operatives southeast toward Jerusalem. They went by the Ben Gurion International Airport, passed through Ramla, and were soon at the Jaffa Gate entrance to Old Jerusalem. The driver pulled into the bus and taxi waiting area and Zivah announced, "Okay. This is one of the main entrances to the Old City. We'll get out here and walk the rest of the way. I'll call the limo driver when we're ready to return to Tel Aviv and he'll pick us up at this very same spot."

"Sounds like a plan," Pat responded. The others nodded in agreement.

The operatives walked through the narrow portal and up David Street. "For those that haven't been here before, David's Tower and the Citadel are on the right," Ari announced as he pointed at the ancient structures.

Pat mentioned, "Yes, I've been there on previous visits to the Holy Land. There's an interesting museum in the Citadel."

Ari acknowledged his comment with a nod.

"The restaurant isn't far … just past the Armenian Quarter and down a side street," Zivah stated.

The group enjoyed a top-quality kosher dairy buffet on

the second floor of The Quarter Café on Tiferet Yisrael Road. "What a fantastic view of the Western Wall, Temple Mount, and the Mount of Olives," Pat exclaimed.

"The panoramic view is certainly a fine accompaniment to our meal. And I believe the quiche was exquisite ... much like in Paris," André added.

Sarah then offered, "I particularly liked the beef barley soup."

"And I liked the salad loaded with raw carrots, cucumbers, and Mediterranean olives ... to maintain my girlish figure," Zivah stated as she smiled impishly and wiggled her torso.

Fatin smiled demurely and added, "I love the smell of the fresh-baked pastries, especially the *surganiot*."

"Those deep-fried jelly doughnuts were too bloody rich for me," Sarah commented.

Ari nodded his approval for everyone's comments and grinned at Zivah's antics. Then he suggested, "Why don't we have a glass of Sabra? It's our delicious national cordial."

"Yes, yes, I love the smooth, aromatic Jaffa orange and chocolate flavor of Sabra," Zivah agreed.

"I understand that Sabra means native-born Israeli," Pat remarked.

Zivah and Ari replied, "Yes it does," in unison.

The operatives strolled back toward Jaffa Gate. As they approached a Jewish tourist shop on David Street near the Citadel, there was a tremendous explosion and the building was blown to bits. "Terrorist bomb," Ari yelled as pieces of glass, brick, stone, and metal flew completely across the crowded street. The seasoned agents instinctively dove for the ground, but Ari had to pull inexperienced Fatin down with him.

"*Sacré Bleu*, I'm hit!" screamed André. Tourists and locals moaned in pain from their injuries as dust and smoke permeated the narrow roadway.

The other five agents, all unscathed, looked at him, and Sarah hollered, "André's head is wounded!" as she reached over and applied pressure to stop the bleeding.

Just then, an Arab wearing a *djellaba* and *keffiyeh* jumped out of a nearby doorway, yelled "*Allah o Akbar*," and started running toward the center of Old Jerusalem.

"That looks like Abdul al-Yemeni," Ari proclaimed.

"It *is* al-Yemeni. Patrick, he's a high-ranking member of the Palestine Liberation Front terrorist group, and Shin Bet's been looking for him. They call him 'The PLF Ghost' because he's so elusive. Let's get him!" Zivah yelled as she drew her Beretta.

"Fatin and Sarah, tend to André's wound. Ari and Zivah, you're with me. Let's go after that 'God is Great' *jihadist*," Pat commanded.

The three operatives were now in a combat mode and running after the terrorist. They chased him along David Street, down The Street of the Chain, and into the Arab *souk*. "We might lose him in this huge bazaar," Zivah declared breathlessly. "A lot of men wear the desert robe and headdress attire in here."

In the lead, Pat yelled, "He turned left at that alley next to the rug shop!"

"He's heading toward the Muslim Quarter," Ari

responded.

The three operatives ran down the constricted alleyway, avoiding produce carts, tables laden with gold necklaces, and a multitude of Arab, Jew, and foreign tourist shoppers.

An Arab wearing a black and white PLO-type headdress stepped out of a doorway in front of the agents and hollered, "*Allah o Akbar,*" as he started to raise a 9-millimeter PP-2000 submachine gun.

Zivah quickly pulled her knife from its sheath and expertly threw it at the man standing twenty feet in front of them. The throwing knife found its mark and penetrated the Arab's heart. He immediately dropped to the ground without firing a shot.

Pat yelled, "Why didn't you just shoot him?"

"Too many innocents around," she replied.

A block later, Pat finally called off the chase. "We lost him. I can see why he's called The PLF Ghost. Let's head back to David Street and see how André is doing."

"You're right, Patrick. We don't want to be poking our heads into any of these Palestinian shops, or we may lose them," Zivah advised soberly.

"I agree," Ari stated.

IDF and Shin Bet investigators milled around the demolished tourist shop, and emergency medical teams tended to the injured. "Zivah, over here," Cailin Rinesmann shouted as the operatives returned to David Street.

Zivah told her IDF childhood friend what happened during and after the blast, including the confrontation with the co-conspirator and the dead man's location.

"Did you know the proprietor was killed in the blast, and

several shoppers were injured?"

"No, I didn't. Another senseless murder of a civilian by a Palestinian terrorist," Zivah murmured while shaking her head.

"The Ghost also dropped this bag of *qat* as he ran off, according to a bystander," Cailin said as she held out a clear plastic bag filled with green leaves for Zivah to observe.

"Patrick, the locals in Yemen chew it as a stimulant, and it gives them a general sense of well-being." Pat nodded in understanding.

"Here Patrick, meet my life-long friend, Cailin."

"Shalom! Cailin. It's my pleasure."

Cailin winked at Zivah with approval as she shook hands with Pat.

Sarah then asked Pat and Ari, "Did you leave him dead in an alley?"

Pat responded, "No, we lost him in the *souk*. He really is like a ghost."

Ari added. "But, Zivah effectively took care of an accomplice in an alley!"

Fatin then advised, "André is okay. Just a glancing blow to the head with a piece of rock."

"*Merci, bon ami*. It's good that my head is harder than the rock!" André exclaimed.

All six agents burst into uncontrollable laughter, relieving the tensions of the blast, André's injury, and the pursuit of The Ghost. The investigators, medics, and onlookers gave them perplexed glances.

As they were leaving the blast scene, Sarah bent over to

pick up a silver-colored ballpoint pen on the sidewalk. Zivah yelled, "Freeze, Sarah! Don't touch it!"

Ari added, "It may be a pen bomb planted by a terrorist group. Stand clear and I'll call the bomb squad over here."

The bomb experts then secured the area. While the group headed for the Jaffa Gate, Sarah confessed, "Wow! I'm shaking. That was a bloody close one. I hope it's not an omen of what's ahead for me."

"That's just part of the job," Pat commented. The others chuckled and nodded in agreement. "Okay, let's all give our agencies an update on the incident."

The others nodded as they retrieved their BlackBerrys.

Tel Aviv

Early the next morning, all three teams reported to the Mossad firing range. Standing side-by-side three meters from their targets, Pat and Zivah held their Uzis at the ready position. The selector switches were set on full-auto and the safeties were off.

"I'm ready for action," Zivah whispered.

Pat nodded and replied, "Okay, fire!"

The operatives leaned into their submachine guns while raising them toward the two dark silhouettes seven meters away, and squeezed their triggers as the front sights neared the targets' torsos. The weapons fired 9-millimeter bullets at 600-rounds-per-minute and emptied the magazines in less than three seconds.

"I've always liked this awesome, close-quarters gun!"

"Me too! It's my favorite weapon. Let's check out the 'Bad Guys,' Patrick."

"Aha! All 25 rounds are in the black on my target."

"My first round hit a millimeter short of the lower left torso on my target. But, the rest of the rounds are in the black," Zivah added.

"That's still good shooting." Pointing at the two cardboard targets, Pat continued, "Look at the identical shot patterns. We both started at the lower left waist area, and held tight as the sub-guns climbed up and to the right during full-auto fire, and our last rounds hit the right shoulder areas of the targets. You can't get any better than that!"

"I agree. I taught the technique that we just used while instructing Shin Bet agents before transferring to Mossad." Smiling at her lover, Zivah continued, "Okay, our pistol qualification is next. Then we'll be ready for our mission assignment."

The two operatives stepped back to the seven-meter line on the Mossad firing range, in front of two fresh targets. "Okay. I'm ready, Zivah."

"On my command, we'll draw our Berettas from the holster, put two rounds in the center of mass, and follow up with one round in the forehead of the silhouettes ... all within five seconds. Ready ... set ... fire!"

They drew and presented their 9-millimeter Berettas quickly and smoothly. The ensuing six shots sounded like three, and the exercise was over in less than four seconds. The operatives then re-holstered their weapons.

"Clear on the firing line! Okay, check our targets, Patrick."

Pat and Zivah examined the targets. There was one large hole in the sternum, and one small hole in the middle of the cranium, on both targets.

"Look! We both placed the first two rounds in one hole. I wondered if you were as good with the pistol as I thought you were. Now, I know you are!"

"Ditto for you, Patrick. Well, we passed our weapons qualifications. I'll give the chief our range results."

"Freeze!" yelled Pat as he quickly drew his pistol. "There's a viper near your left foot, but it's too close to you for me to make a safe shot. I'll try to get it to strike at me while you dispatch it." He then took a step in the direction of the venomous snake and waved his left hand to entice it toward him.

Meanwhile, Zivah took a step backward and drew her pistol. She then took a step to the right and carefully aimed at the snake's head before it could strike at Pat. The 115 grain hollow point bullet completely shattered the snake's head, and Zivah exclaimed, "That was a Palestinian Viper, and they are the leading cause of deadly snakebites in Israel and the West Bank."

"Good shooting. If the others are ready, let's head back to HQ," Pat suggested.

Chapter Three: West Bank

Tel Aviv

Ariel Mazar opened the meeting with, "Team One has a top priority assignment. Agents Benjamin and O'Leary will seek out and apprehend 'The PLF Ghost' ... dead or alive!" Motioning toward a PowerPoint map displayed on a wall screen, she continued, "Intel makes us believe Abdul al-Yemeni is in Ramallah as we speak, so start there. He certainly lives up to his reputation as The PLF Ghost, so he probably won't still be in Ramallah when you arrive. Your assignment is to find him, no matter where he goes or how long it takes. Remember this, others have tried to apprehend al-Yemeni and failed. Some of those agents met horrible fates, so be careful."

"What happened to them?" Pat asked.

"They were beheaded by the PLF terrorists," Ariel responded quietly.

With a pained expression, Zivah added, "One of them, Golda Bachmann, was a dear friend of mine, Patrick."

Grimacing, Pat nodded in sympathy.

"You are to be deployed to the West Bank effective ASAP. Take your Uzis, Brettas, plenty of magazines, and extra ammunition. Remember, this is a dangerous assignment, and the Palestinian Liberation Front has ears everywhere. So use your BlackBerrys for cryptic text messages only, and be sure to include me in all transmittals. Also, I've sent photos of al-Yemeni to your BlackBerrys. Wear Kevlar T-shirts under your outer wear. They will at least stop handgun rounds and may save your life."

Reaching into her briefcase, Mazar pulled out two plain envelopes. "Here are 35,000 shekels for each of you. That's equivalent to about $10,000 U.S. apiece. The money is to be used for your expenses, and for payments to local informants and contacts. Spend it like it's your money, because you are accountable to *me* for each and every shekel."

"Will do, Chief," Pat replied.

Zivah nodded in assent.

Ramallah

It was a warm day as Pat and Zivah headed north out of modern Jerusalem on the Old Damascus Road. Puffy white clouds floated across the blue sky from the Mediterranean Sea, projecting dancing shadows on the barren desert floor. Pat was driving an older 1990s vintage Ford Mustang, with green Palestinian Authority license plates, toward the Israeli-West Bank frontier. Two stern-faced border guards took their Mossad identification cards and handed them to an IDF colonel. The tall, dark-complexioned officer approached their vehicle and exclaimed with a big grin, "Zivah, dear Zivah! It's been a while since I've seen you. We miss you at IDF."

Oh, oh! That handsome devil must be one of Zivah's old boyfriends, Pat surmised.

Zivah removed her black headscarf as she got out of the car, embraced the officer, and commented, "Cousin Abraham, I see you're going up through the ranks!"

"Yes, I'm in line for general now. Maybe someday soon!"

"Good for you! I wish you the best." Motioning toward Pat, she whispered, "This is my *very* special friend, CIA Agent Patrick O'Leary. He's on loan to Mossad, and we're hunting for The PLF Ghost."

The colonel handed their IDs to Zivah and advised quietly, "I hear he's in Ramallah now. But, he may not be there for long." Pointing at his guards, he ordered, "Let them through!"

"Yes, we know how elusive The Ghost is." Pat waved at Abraham as they drove through the gate in the high frontier wall. "Wherever he goes, we will be right behind him." Then he confessed to Zivah, "I was worried that the colonel was an old boyfriend."

"Patrick, Dear, you know I'm all yours," she replied demurely. Zivah's pearly-white teeth sparkled in the bright sunlight as she donned her scarf and smiled at Pat.

It was just a few more miles to the hills of Ramallah, the "Height of God." They could see tall, sand-colored church bell towers and mosque minarets while approaching the administrative capital of the Palestinian National Authority.

"You may know that Ramallah was once a predominately Christian town. Today, it's dominated by Muslims. However, the city still has a strong Christian population."

"I understand that it was named by Arab Christians that migrated here from Jordan during the 16th century. Today, it's also a sister city of Muscatine, Iowa. Perhaps we'll have a few friends here," Pat replied.

"We do. More than a few."

The six-mile trip from Jerusalem to Ramallah through ocher-hued rolling hills took about twenty minutes.

Just past the Melkite Catholic Church, Zivah said, "Patrick, stop next to that teahouse on the right. Our local informant should be waiting there for our arrival."

41

As Pat and Zivah sat down at an outdoor table and ordered hot tea, a Palestinian Arab dressed in traditional *djellaba* and *keffiyeh* Arab clothing approached them. Pat immediately went into Condition Black, ready for combat with the enemy.

The Arab sat down at a nearby table and ordered tea.

Zivah smiled at the man and greeted him softly with, *"As salam' alakoom, Adib"*

Pat then relaxed, but contemplated, *I don't know if we can trust this chap.*

Speaking perfect English, with a slight British accent, Adib responded quietly to her Arabic greeting, with "Cheerio, Zivah. How are you this fine day?"

"Very well, thank you." She introduced Pat, and asked softy, "Do you know where we can find The PLF Ghost, Adib?"

"I just heard on the street that he was at the tomb of Yasser Arafat this morning, but has since left for Nablus," he replied while observing her alluring body.

Zivah handed Adib 350 shekels under the table as they finished their tea.

Walking back to the Mustang, Pat murmured, "One hundred bucks is a lot for finding out what we already expected would happen. What will Director Mazar say about that?"

"She knows Adib is a good informant, and we always pay him well." Holding her hand out for the car keys, she continued, "I know the Palestinian Territory, Patrick, so I'll drive." A mournful call to prayer emitted from a neighborhood mosque minaret as she pulled away from the teahouse.

Nablus

Zivah headed northeast on the Jerusalem-Nablus Highway. Winding through mountains of the Samaria region, the operatives went past shepherds minding fat-tailed sheep munching on sparse, low-growing foliage on the barren hillsides. Then they drove by rows of planted crops in small valleys waiting for the next rainfall to germinate the seeds.

"You know, Patrick, this was a very productive agricultural region before we turned over the West Bank to the Palestinian National Authority a few years back."

"Yep, I remember touring the territory during the Israeli occupation after the Six-day War. It was really a booming region then. Although, the shepherds and their sheep look the same today ... as if they were frozen in time."

"Just as they did two or three thousand years ago, Patrick."

They drove through the towns of Silwad, Qabalan, Awarta, and several small villages where there were IDF checkpoints. Approaching Nablus, nestled on a knoll between Mount Ebal and Mount Gerizing, Zivah advised, "Mossad has a contact here who runs a lamb kebab stand by the Nablus Bazaar. We'll stop there and find out what he knows."

"Good. I'm getting hungry anyway."

The thirty-mile trip from Ramallah took over an hour because of the checkpoint delays. Driving past the Great Mosque of Nablus, Zivah mentioned, "This edifice was once a Crusader church, and a mosque before the Crusades."

"The region certainly has a fascinating history."

Walking up to the kebab cart, the operatives smelled the mingled aromas of bazaar spices, fresh-baked flatbread, and grilled lamb. Zivah exclaimed, "Now, *I'm* getting hungry!"

She then greeted the vendor, handed him 350 shekels neatly folded up, and quietly ordered, "Two kebabs in flatbread please, Abdullah. And, the whereabouts of The PLF Ghost."

Handing Zivah the kebabs, the Palestinian looked around cautiously and responded in broken English, "He walk to *souk*, *Madame*, but not there for long."

Pat whispered, "Zivah, I can't believe you're discussing this in front of an Arab *souk*!"

"It's okay. Sometimes it's better to hide what we're doing in plain sight."

Just then, Abdullah anxiously announced, "Look, look! He out of *souk* now."

Pat and Zivah dropped their kebabs as they spun around to look for The Ghost, and they spotted him as he was getting into the backseat of a maroon Mercedes-Benz sedan. Pat hollered, "Shoot, shoot!"

The two operatives swiftly drew their silencer-fitted Berettas and fired at the vehicle until their magazines were empty as it pulled away from the curb. They immediately made tactical reloads as the Mercedes sped away and turned up a side street.

"Zivah, run for the Mustang!" Sprinting toward their vehicle, Pat continued, "I think all thirty of our rounds hit his car. It's riddled with bullet holes, and hopefully a few slugs hit al-Yemeni."

"I sure hope you're right, Patrick!" Rubbing her stomach, she added, "Looks like we'll skip lunch today." After jumping into their car, they drove past Jacob's Well at high speed and were soon in hot pursuit of Abdul al-Yemeni. The Mercedes headed northeast and Zivah declared, "He's going toward Tubas."

"I don't know if this old Ford can catch up with the Mercedes."

"They're driving a diesel, Patrick, and may have trouble picking up speed again after slowing down for the hilly curves ahead. We can catch up to them then."

"With your superb driving skills, and this hot little Mustang, we can do it! I'd better give Chief Mazar an update," *in hot pursuit toward tubas. viper.* "I'll give my CIA chief an incident report later."

The Palestinians were about a half mile ahead of them going into a curve when the driver slowed down. However, when he floor-boarded it after coming out of the curve, the sluggish diesel engine struggled to get back up to speed.

Zivah used engine compression to slow down going into the curve, and then punched it in the middle of the turn. The vehicle hugged the road and shot forward as they came out of it.

"See what I mean? We're only a quarter of a mile from them now."

"Good driving! We'll catch up to them after the next bend or two," Pat replied.

A bullet suddenly ripped through the top of the Mustang's windshield and blew apart the rear view mirror. "The Ghost is shooting at us with a machine pistol. It looks like a Czechoslovakian Skorpion." While taking the safety off his Uzi and setting the selector switch to full-auto, Pat continued, "I'll return fire when we go into the next right-hand curve."

Approaching Tamun, they went into a left-hand curve, so Pat didn't have an opportunity to shoot at the Mercedes. However, they were only a sixteenth of a mile behind their prey when the Mustang pulled out of the turn.

"Right-hand curve coming up Patrick. Remember our firing range session!" She geared down going into it and said, "He's yours now, now!"

Pat leaned out the right window, held the Uzi tight, sighted in on the left rear tire of the Mercedes, and squeezed the trigger. A few seconds later, making a tactical reload, he dropped the empty magazine on the road and inserted a full one in the submachine gun.

Pat yelled to overcome the high-speed wind noise of the chase, "I think all twenty five rounds hit the vehicle. The driver must be injured because the vehicle's out of control. Maybe I hit The Ghost! Now that wasn't bad shooting while moving was it?"

The Mercedes ran off the road and down an embankment. Zivah screeched to a halt on the roadway and Pat yelled, "They're stuck in a *wadi* at the bottom of the ravine. Let's go down and get the 'God is Great' *jihadist*."

A group of sheepherders gathered around the Mercedes as Pat and Zivah scrambled down the steep ravine slope. While the shepherds were pulling out the dead driver, Zivah hollered, "Look. The Ghost is gone! There's no one else in the vehicle."

Apparently intimidated by the two Uzi-armed operatives, the shepherds ran up and out of the ravine in various directions.

"I speculate he really is a ghost," Pat offered.

"And maybe he disappeared with the shepherds. Hurry, back to our car Patrick. We want to *greet* him when he arrives at Tubas. Then we can send him to *Sheol*."

"Good strategy. Then he'll be in Hades with the other

dead *jihadists*. I'll update the chief while you drive." *high-speed firefight. driver dead. ghost escaped. viper.*

Mazar instantly replied, *better get him next time! bushmaster.*

Tubas

Zivah drove swiftly up the winding road, and through the barren ocher-hued hills of the sun-drenched Samaria region. Forested peaks, planted crops, and a view of the Jordan Valley greeted them as they neared Tubas. "You should have been a racecar driver," Pat commented.

"Just proving I can drive as well as you, Dear! Just kidding ... we must get to Tubas before The Ghost."

"No need to tell *you* to step on it!"

"Did you know this city was once called Thebez?" Zivah asked. "It was a Canaanite town in Old Israel centuries ago."

"No, I didn't know that. Thebez is briefly mentioned in the Old Testament. Wasn't it the site of a revolt?"

"That's correct. Which reminds me, I want you to explain more about Christianity and the New Testament. I'm curious about your religion."

"It will be my pleasure ... sometime when we're on R&R," Pat replied as Zivah turned left onto the first main boulevard in town. She made a U-turn, and parked the Mustang in the shade near the highway.

"This is perfect, Zivah. It gives us a view of anyone coming into town from the south ... without them seeing us."

"Now we wait. I'm hungry. It's too bad we dropped our kebabs when we spotted al-Yemeni back in Nablus."

"Yep. I'm also famished. We'll have to settle on drinking

our water."

Zivah then sent Mazar a text, *in position. cobra.*

Ariel Mazar replied, *idf commandos on alert at nearby base. text if backup needed. bushmaster.*

A half-hour later, Pat exclaimed, "Look! That's Adib driving past in a 1960s vintage Chevrolet Malibu. What's he doing here?"

"I see him. There's a passenger wearing shepherd's clothing crouched down in the back seat. Maybe it's The Ghost!"

As Zivah pulled onto the highway to follow the Chevy into town, Pat exclaimed, "I had a bad feeling about Adib back in Ramallah. I didn't think he could be trusted. In fact, he's much too intelligent to be a mere informant."

"It would surprise me, but he just may be a double-agent. We'll find out when we stop their vehicle. But, not until we have to, because Hamas is active in Tubas and they have close ties to the PLF. The Ghost may even be in touch with them now. I hope he's heading for Jenin and won't stop here. Then we can confront them on the open highway."

"Good plan, Zivah. We certainly don't want a firefight with Hamas in front of the Palestinian authorities. Stay at least a hundred yards behind them going through town and they might not spot us."

"Okay. I know we're in a precarious position." The Chevy continued north through town, past the Palestinian National Authority's Tubas Governorate Headquarters, then by the Holy Trinity Orthodox Church on the north side. "Patrick, there's only 60 Palestinian Christians here ... in a city of 16,000 Muslims," Zivah stated as she pointed at the church.

"The Christians are certainly outnumbered in this town."

"As well as in the rest of the West Bank. Many Christians have left the area."

A minute later, Pat advised, "It *does* look like they're heading out of Tubas toward Jenin. I'll text the chief and ask for IDF support now. Maybe they can set up a roadblock on the highway." *bushmaster. need roadblock south of al-zababidah. tout de suite. adib chauffeuring the ghost. viper.*

Ariel Mazar replied in a few seconds, *done. adib must be double agent. bushmaster.*

As they left the city, Zivah floored the Mustang. "We'll catch them now. They can't outrun us with that old rickety Chevy."

"Incoming RPG!" Pat screamed. "Swerve left! Swerve left!"

Zivah swerved into the southbound lane and a rocket propelled grenade exploded in the northbound lane near their right rear fender. Shrapnel from the high explosive warhead peppered the fender and trunk lid, and the concussion force pushed the Mustang's rear end to the left. Zivah struggled to keep control, and finally straightened out the vehicle. "Wow! That was a near miss. I can feel that we still have all four tires intact, and we're not losing fuel so the gas tank is okay," she exclaimed.

"Zigzag until we're out of RPG range. Damned Hamas terrorists!"

"My hands are shaking, but will do."

"Okay, we're out of range. Great driving! Step on it, Zivah. They must know we're in hot pursuit now."

Zivah was catching up to the Chevy as they sped up the

barren hill. "Maybe IDF will set up a roadblock just over the crest of this grade. That would certainly surprise Adib and The Ghost because they wouldn't see it until it was too late."

Just then, Ariel Mazar sent a text message, *roadblock setup on highway downgrade to al-zababidah. bushmaster.*

"As they say in the States, "You've hit the nail on the head!" Pat commented with a grin. At 110 miles-per-hour, the two operatives quickly closed in on the Chevy. "The light Mustang will be airborne at this speed, if we hit a deep *wadi* crossing the road."

"I know the road, and I can gear down before that happens, Patrick."

When the operatives were within a few car lengths of the Chevy, the rear seat passenger stuck his arm out the window and opened fire on them with a full-automatic weapon. "He's shooting his 9-mill Skorpion, but he can't aim at us on this straight-away when we're right behind him. Now I know it's The Ghost," Pat yelled as he returned fire with his Uzi set on full-auto. Most of Pat's rounds hit the trunk of the Chevy, and a few shattered the rear window.

The two vehicles were nearly bumper-to-bumper when they reached the crest of the hill. "Our Mustang is too small to spin them out by ramming the right side of their rear bumper."

"I agree, Zivah. We would be the ones to spin out. That's a California Highway Patrol maneuver, and they use heavy cruisers."

"Look! *Sayeret Matkal* set up roadblock a few hundred yards down the hill. We've got them now," Zivah exclaimed.

Adib immediately slammed on his brakes and started to make a U-turn. However, Zivah also braked fast and pulled sideways across the middle of the highway to block their escape. "Get out! Get out! He's going to T-bone us," Pat screamed as the Chevy headed straight toward his passenger door.

Pat immediately jumped out, and Zivah dove out behind him. While stunned on the ground, the impact nearly pushed the Mustang on top of the two operatives, but they managed to quickly roll away from the vehicle.

With the Uzis still in the Mustang, Pat and Zivah quickly drew their Berettas as they stood up and faced the wrecked vehicles. They were in a combat mode, with fingers on the triggers of their pistols. "I'll take the left," Zivah yelled.

"I'm on the right. Careful!" Meanwhile the commandos drove up to the scene and deployed in a circle around the wrecked vehicles.

"Freeze, Adib! Hands on the steering wheel! Now!" Zivah yelled.

Adib, covered with blood and bleeding profusely from a head wound, didn't move. He murmured, "Sorry, Zivah, I had to do ..." as he expired.

Pat approached the other side of the Chevy and yelled, "Get out now, Abdul! With your hands up." Not getting a response, Pat stood to one side with his weapon at the ready position as he cautiously opened the rear door. "The Ghost is gone!"

"Everyone spread out and search the hills," Zivah yelled at the commandos. "He has to be hiding close by!"

"Check every crevice, cave, depression, and *wadi*, and behind every rock, bush, and tumbleweed," Pat added.

"Do it!" the commando team leader, Lieutenant Aaron Meir, ordered.

51

The commandos and the two operatives carefully searched the area until dusk, but couldn't find Abdul al-Yemeni. The PLF Ghost had vanished again! Zivah reluctantly updated Mazar with a text message.

i said to get him this time! it's your last chance now. i will replace you with team two if you fail again. bushmaster, Mazar instantly replied.

"Wow! The chief is *very* irate!" Zivah announced. She then read the message to Pat.

"Okay. Set up observation sites along the highway from Tubas to al-Zababidah. Man them all night and until midday tomorrow," Lieutenant Meir instructed his commandos.

"It's imperative that we catch The PLF Ghost … dead or alive," Zivah added. "Preferably dead," she murmured softly. "Patrick, it's only about 20 miles to Afula, across the border in Israel. We will be safer spending the night there and returning at daybreak."

"Great idea. The Mustang is totaled, so let's borrow one of the IDF Storms. I'll inform the chief." *moving to safe haven. returning in the morning to resume search. viper.*

approved. bushmaster, Ariel Mazar replied to Pat's message.

"I guess she's calmed down, at least a little bit," Pat informed Zivah.

The two operatives headed north with Pat at the wheel of the military Jeep-type vehicle. They passed through darkened al-Zababidah and then bustling Jenin. When the pair reached the West Bank-Israel frontier, the border guards waved them through the checkpoint into Israel. An IDF captain hollered, "*Shalom,* Zivah. The commander said to expect you. See you on your way back in the morning." She winked knowingly, grinned as she waved at the two operatives, and nodded approvingly at Pat.

Zivah returned the salutation, and Pat hollered *Shalom!* Cailin."

Pat and Zivah checked into Kibbutz Mira Country Lodging near Afula in the Valley of Jezreel. After showering, they enjoyed a much-needed meal of kosher beef stew and unleavened flatbread at the dining room. "Let's top off this delicious feast with a glass of Sabra," Zivah suggested.

"Sounds good to me. I love the flavor of your national after-dinner liqueur, and it will help us unwind."

The couple retired after finishing their drinks, and instantly fell asleep in each other's arms.

~~~

The operatives woke before dawn. "Let's grab some fruit and flatbread at the kibbutz dining hall," Zivah suggested. "We'll have our breakfast on the road."

"Right. We want to resume the search for The PLF Ghost at daybreak."

Pat sped south on the highway. The Israeli frontier guards saluted and waved them on into the West Bank, and Pat didn't slow down at all going through the barricade gate.

A *muezzin's* melodic call to prayer emitted from a minaret at the off-white colored Fatima Khatun Mosque as they drove into Jenin. "That's the first of the five daily calls to prayer, Patrick."

"I know, the five daily prayers are called the *Namez* in Iran, and I assume in the Arab countries as well."

"That's correct. *Namez* is an Arabic word."

After passing through the bright green Samarian hills and dells of Jenin, they went by the drab, stark-looking Jenin Refugee Camp. The operatives stopped at the first commando post just south of al-Zababidah as the sun peeked over Biblical Mount Hermon.

"*Shalom!*" the lone commando greeted them.

"*Shalom!*" Pat and Zivah responded in unison.

"Abdul al-Yemeni has not yet surfaced between here and our first outlook post just north of Tubas. He may have left the area during the night."

The commando's tactical radio crackled, and then a voice commanded, "Attention! Attention! This is Lieutenant Meir. Sentry Three at the crest of the hill has not responded to my check-in calls. Everyone report to the site immediately!"

"Jump in!" Zivah yelled as she opened the Storm's door for the commando. Pat then headed up the steep grade at full-throttle. They stopped at the crest of the hill as Lieutenant Aaron Meir and the rest of his commando team arrived.

"Quick! Up to that boulder," Meir ordered as he pointed to a huge rock on a ledge above the road. "That's Corporal Rabin's post."

The commandos and the two operatives scrambled up the steep slope. Pat reached the boulder first with his Beretta drawn

. "Oh, no, the corporal's throat's been cut and he bled out!" he exclaimed.

"He's been dead for awhile," Lieutenant Meir yelled as he checked Corporal Rabin for a pulse. Meir radioed the IDF base for helicopter support to search the surrounding desert. "Bring infrared equipment. ASAP. We must find al-Yemeni before the blazing sun heats up the desert floor and makes the infrared gear useless," he advised Base Operations.

"Roger. ETA ten minutes," Operations responded.

Four Blackhawk helicopters converged on the scene and began searching the surrounding desolate wilderness. Meanwhile, Pat, Zivah, and the commando team scoured the hilltop. At mid-morning, when the heat from the sun-scorched desert sands rendered the equipment unusable, Lieutenant Meir called off the search. "The infrared equipment only picked up a herd of sheep and a lone shepherd," he explained.

Pat and Zivah looked at each other knowingly. "Damn it! That was probably The PLF Ghost," Pat responded.

"I'd better give the chief the bad news," Zivah said reluctantly.

"I hope Mazar's over her anger and won't replace us like she threatened to do. I really want this guy now, and I'll personally send him directly to Hell when we catch him," Pat avowed.

"We'll send him to *Sheol* together, Patrick." Zivah then sent Mazar a text message on her BlackBerry, *ghost disappeared again. one commando slain. need new vehicle to continue pursuit. cobra.*

Ariel Mazar instantly replied, *intel reports ghost may head for gaza via jericho & hebron. must be stopped, repeat must be stopped, before he gets to gaza. vehicle on way from local idf base. bushmaster.*

"Great! The chief must be over her anger at us. Here, read her text."

Pat read the message and commented, "What a relief. It looks like we're heading south as soon as our new vehicle arrives."

"You know, Patrick, it's too bad the PLF, Hamas, Hezbollah, and the other Palestinian terrorist groups didn't accept Yasser Arafat's 'Declaration of Principles' document he signed in 1993. If they had, we wouldn't be fighting this battle now!"

"Wasn't that the paper Chairman Arafat signed to recognize the right of the State of Israel to exist in peace and security?"

"You're absolutely right. All this senseless murder and mayhem over the past two decades should not have happened." Zivah paused a moment, then continued, "Moreover, the Palestinians would have had their own state by now, consisting of the West Bank and Gaza Strip, *if* they had accepted the PLO's declaration."

A few minutes later, a 2000 Renault Clio Sport sedan, equipped with Palestinian Authority license plates, arrived at the top of the grade. A handsome young IDF private jumped out of the vehicle and handed the keys to Zivah. "Agent Benjamin, this old French car may not look fast, but it is. Our motor pool sergeant souped-up the V-6 engine and it can outrun most other cars around here," the private declared. Handing Pat a black case, he added, "Agent O'Leary, Mossad Chief Mazar told me to deliver this new state-of-the-art binocular system to you."

"Good. We need a change of luck. Maybe this is it," Pat replied. "Let's go get that bloody *jihadist!*"

Jericho

Zivah drove the Renault through Tubas and turned left on the Old Jericho Road. Heading southeast, she explained, "That's Wadi al Fariah we're following on the right."

"I know. I've traveled this road before. Doesn't the dry

wadi end at the Jordan River?"

"It does. You do know my region very well." She picked up speed on a long straight away and exclaimed, "Wow! The private was right ... this old car *is* powerful."

The highway crossed over the *wadi* and headed due south. They drove past Israeli farm fields with crop seedlings covered with plastic sheets to preserve moisture in the soil. Palestinian Arabs were tending flocks of sheep on the Jordan Valley hillsides. "We're approaching Jericho, Patrick."

"Yes, I see the remains of the ancient walls at Tel Jericho. If I remember correctly, many thousands of years ago Joshua's troops marched around the walled city and blew their trumpets for seven days. I believe the walls then tumbled down."

"That was during the Israelite invasion of Canaan, God's Promised Land for the Jews, during their exodus from Egypt." After a short pause, she commented, "Patrick, we just left Samaria, the northern part of the West Bank, and are now in Judea, the southern part of the territory." They entered a green-belt agricultural area in the Jericho desert oasis and Zivah slowed down as they approached the Jerusalem-Amman Road in town. "I'll park behind that date stand across the highway. We can observe this intersection from the shade inside the stand, and we won't be seen behind those long bunches of dates hanging in front."

"Good idea. If we do spot The Ghost, we'll have to get to our vehicle as quickly as possible," Pat commented.

Standing in the cool shadows of the date stand, the operatives snacked on sweet, chewy, and aromatic deep-brown Medjool dates offered by the Arab vendor. "Did you know Jericho is more than 10,000 years old?" Zivah asked Pat.

"Yep. I stopped at this very date stand many years ago,

tasted the dates, and explored the town and the twenty levels of civilization at the archeological dig. Jericho has quite a history. I'd better update the chief."

"Quick, look at that dusty white Mercedes delivery truck coming into town on the Old Jericho Road."

Wearing an electroencephalogram cap, Pat focused his CT_2WS brainwave binoculars on the vehicle as it turned right onto the Jerusalem-Amman Road. He instantly described the occupants, "The driver is an older Arab with brown eyes, bad teeth, wrinkled facial skin with a dark mole on his left cheek, and white beard and moustache. He's wearing a *djellaba* and *keffiyeh*. The passenger is a much younger Arab with dark ghoulish eyes, smooth facial skin, a dark beard, and he's wearing shepherds' clothing. That one certainly looks like Abdul al-Yemeni."

"The Ghost, Patrick, The Ghost!" Zivah yelled. "Quick, run for the car."

"I'm right behind you. You'd better drive in case they take a road I'm not familiar with. I'll text Mazar."

Driving onto the pavement, Zivah exclaimed, "That new binocular system certainly provided your brain with immediate information!"

As Pat stowed the EEG cap and binoculars, he replied, "Yes, the U.S. military calls it the 'Luke Skywalker Binocular System' because it taps into the brain and provides instant information on everything picked up by the binoculars. It greatly improves observations."

The Mercedes driver headed west into the Judean Wilderness on the Jericho-Jerusalem Road, with Pat and Zivah in hot pursuit. Awestruck at the desert chase scene, dozens of colorfully dressed Bedouin nomads stood in front of their huge black goat hair tents and stared at the two vehicles. They whizzed past Joshua's Fortress positioned high above the road on a rocky cliff, and The Inn of the Good Samaritan, as Zivah began to close in on their prey. "We've got him now!" she exclaimed.

"Maybe, Zivah, maybe." Just below the Mount of Temptation, Abdul al-Yemeni, opened one of the rear doors of the truck and pointed his Skorpion at them. "Duck," Pat yelled as a dozen 9-millimeter bullets ripped through the windshield and roof of the Renault.

Zivah crisscrossed the highway evasively as Pat kicked out the shattered windshield. He then returned fire with his Uzi set on full-auto. The Ghost shut the rear door and the driver swerved from shoulder to shoulder. Pat managed to pepper the vehicle with rounds from his Uzi, but their quarry continued down the road at high speed. "Zivah, one thing about Mercedes ... they always put powerful engines in their vehicles."

"I'm shaking a lot now, Patrick. But, that *jihadist* is mine!

Bethlehem

Avoiding collisions with occasional slow automobiles and oncoming traffic in the hills, the two vehicles quickly approached Bethany just south of Jerusalem and then drove past Shepherd's Field on the outskirts of Bethlehem. Pat sent a text message to Chief Mazar, *running firefight with ghost on highway. approaching bethlehem from east. need assistance. viper.*

Mazar responded quickly, *sending team two for backup at solomons pools & idf troops to mamre. they have description. ghost getting to close to gaza. must not let him get on highway to the sea at mamre or past hebron. bushmaster.*

Pat read the message to Zivah as they sped past the Basilica of the Nativity. "I can't shoot at them now, Zivah.

Too many innocents on the streets."

Nodding in agreement, she declared, "I hope Ari and Sarah make it to Solomon's Pools before we do, in case we *don't* catch up to The Ghost."

"So do I ... so do I." Al-Yemeni began shooting at the operatives again when they were almost out of Bethlehem. Pat returned fire when they were heading south on the divided Beersheba-Nazareth Road and clear of the multitude of pilgrims and locals in town.

"We're on the 'Way of the Patriarchs' now, Patrick. But, I'm going to take the new Bypass Freeway and try to get ahead of The Ghost. Meanwhile, we'll lose sight of his truck temporarily because of the high anti-sniper walls on both sides of the bypass."

"Team Two better be waiting for him at Solomon's Pools! I'll text our route to the chief." After sending the text to Mazar, he added, "The bypass wasn't here the last time I was in the West Bank. I know it parallels the old highway, but isn't it restricted to vehicles with yellow Israeli plates?"

"Yes. It was constructed to protect Israelis from terrorist attacks in the West Bank and to reduce friction with the Palestinians. But, the chief will make sure were okay on the bypass with our green Palestinian Authority license plates."

Just then, Pat received a text from Sarah, *eta Solomon pools 5 min. coral.*

He replied, *on bypass. eta also 5 min. ghost heading south on old highway. viper.*

Zivah took the King Solomon's Pools freeway exit and stopped at the Beersheba-Nazareth Road as Pat received a text from Sarah, *viper. right behind you. coral.*

"Ari and Sarah are right behind us," Pat advised Zivah.

"Lock and load!" They exited the car, and took up combat positions behind it with their Uzis set on full-auto as Team Two arrived to back them up.

Ari and Sarah took battle positions near their vehicle. Pat put on the EEG cap and scanned the highway to the north with the binoculars. "Here he comes! The Ghost has a huge escort, and I can see him grinning from ear to ear! There must be 25 or 30 combatants protecting him. We're out manned so let them by. Zivah, inform the chief."

"Where in the world did they come from?" asked Sarah.

"Who knows? This *is* al-Yemeni's turf. He must have picked them up along the way," Zivah offered. She immediately received a reply from Mazar, *idf ready at mamre & meitar. box them in. bushmaster.*

A caravan of vehicles sped by the intersection, all with Palestinian flags flying in the wind. There were two non-descript pickup trucks in the lead, and two more in the rear, both filled with heavily armed Palestinian Liberation Front fighters wearing black and white *keffiyehs*. The white Mercedes delivery truck in the middle was flanked by a black SUV on each side.

"Here we go!" Zivah shouted. "The IDF is waiting for them with roadblocks down the road and the chief told us to box them in."

Hebron

The four operatives followed the PLF caravan south at 75 miles an hour. They stayed out of range of accurate small arms fire as they went past Rachel's Tomb located near the highway, and then by the Rock of Ages sitting high on a hill. Passing through Halhul, Zivah alerted Pat, "We're getting close to Mamre now."

Looking ahead with the EEG binoculars, Pat exclaimed, "Damn it! The roadblock is set up on a side road ... not the on the Hebron Highway."

"That's to stop The Ghost from taking the Mamre-Ashkelon Highway toward the Mediterranean, where he could then head south to Gaza. There's an IDF security checkpoint just down the highway at Meitar. We'll box him in there."

"I sure hope so. The IDF better have plenty of troops ready!" Pat responded.

As the PLF caravan approached the Meitar checkpoint, two combatants standing in the bed of the first lead pickup truck leaned over the cab roof and pointed Yasin RPGs at the barricade. The IDF personnel retreated from the location just as two grenades were launched at them. The wood and steel barricade, and a nearby military Storm vehicle, exploded into small pieces when hit by the 40-millimeter grenades.

"They fired high explosive anti-tank warheads!" Zivah exclaimed. "Those RPGs are made by Hamas in the Gaza Strip." IDF troops then fired full automatic weapons at the oncoming caravan of PLF vehicles.

"Friendly fire! Friendly fire! Slow down and pullover to the side so we're out of harm's way!" Pat yelled. Zivah immediately followed Pat's instructions. Ari, driving the backup team's vehicle, realized what was going on and did the same.

The first pickup took the brunt of the IDF rounds, crashed into a concrete abutment, and exploded in flames. The second pickup crashed through the debris of the destroyed barricade and ran head-on into an armored personnel carrier. The IDF forces riddled the truck with small arms fire and killed all the surviving occupants.

"Great! The Ghost is now down to four escorts," Pat advised as he watched the scene through the EEG binoculars. "One of the SUVs pulled in front of the Mercedes delivery truck, and the other behind it. They're going to try getting through single file. Will the IDF let *us* through if they make it?"

"Yes, they have descriptions of our vehicles."

Taking heavy fire, the five remaining PLF vehicles sped through the narrow opening of the destroyed barricade. The lead SUV, the Mercedes, and the rear SUV made it through, although all were riddled with bullet holes.

"The IDF took out the last two pickup trucks with rockets. But, the other vehicles are still heading for Hebron," Pat informed Zivah as he sent Mazar an update text message. Zivah stepped on the gas and sped through the destroyed checkpoint barricade. Ari followed right behind her.

While approaching the Hebron Hills, two Sikorsky S-70 Blackhawk helicopters flew over the operatives and fired rockets at the PLF caravan. The rear SUV exploded when hit.

"Those are *Sayeret Matkal* choppers. They may have counter-terrorism commandos onboard," Zivah advised.

"Good! We can certainly use *their* help. The Ghost has just one SUV escorting him now and it's looking better for us, so let's go in for the kill." Entering Hebron, nestled in the Judean Mountains, Pat fired his Uzi at the Mercedes delivery truck as it went by the Tombs of the Patriarchs and Matriarchs. Then he advised Zivah, "I can't shoot anymore. There's a lot of innocents on the streets. Just keep up with them."

Meanwhile, Ariel Mazar notified both teams, *sm boots on ground at highway south edge of town. bushmaster.*

The operatives' vehicles took heavy AK-47 fire from four PLF combatants standing in front of the Hebron Bazaar, and both vehicles were hit by multiple 7.62-millimeter rounds. Pat sent text messages to Ari and Sarah, *do not return fire. to many civilians. viper*. They continued their pursuit of The Ghost, and the bazaar combatants jumped on motorcycles and pursued the operatives.

Zivah sped down the narrow, twisting streets of Old Hebron and Pat messaged Team Two, *get them off our tails. viper*.

Ari made a quick highway patrol U-turn at an intersection and came to an abrupt stop facing the pursuers. He and Sarah exited the automobile and, using the open doors for cover, fired multiple short bursts from their Uzis at the oncoming cyclists. The operatives took out all of the adversaries as they neared their vehicle.

"Four more terrorists down," yelled Ari.

Sarah added, "More bloody *jihadists* go to bloody Hell."

The SM commando contingent fired a Negev light machinegun at the remaining SUV escorting The Ghost when it approached the south side city limits. Hit with dozens of 5.56-millimeter rounds, it plowed into a parked vehicle, flipped over, and exploded. No one survived.

"We've got him now!" Zivah exclaimed.

"It's not over 'til it's over," Pat replied.

The driver of the Mercedes delivery truck transporting The Ghost skidded to a stop, and then backed up and into an alley, stopping next to a teahouse. The Ghost jumped out and fired at Pat and Zivah's Renault as it approached, emptying his Skorpion machine pistol's 20-round magazine. Meanwhile, his driver fired an AK-47 at Ari and Sarah's vehicle not far behind the Renault.

"Quick ... pull over for cover in back of that small moving van," Pat advised.

Their vehicle was hit by several 9-millimeter rounds before Zivah slid to a stop behind the van. Ari then stopped his vehicle behind them. The four operatives jumped out and returned fire with their Uzis set on full-auto.

The Ghost reloaded and fired a short burst toward Sarah. She screamed in pain and yelled, "Blimey! I'm bloody hit!" as she fell to the ground.

Ari ran over to her. "She took two rounds to the vest over her bosom and one in the neck. I think it nicked the right aorta," he shouted while applying pressure to the neck wound.

"Take care of her, Ari! We'll deal with The Ghost," Pat responded. "Zivah, selector switch on single shot. Go for the head. You take out al-Yemeni and I'll take out the driver."

Pat and Zivah fired their Uzis simultaneously and each killed the targets at 25 yards with one well placed 9-millimeter round to their craniums.

"I did it! I killed Abdul al-Yemeni! He's finally in *Sheol*, where he belongs," Zivah yelled for all to hear.

"And, I finished off his driver. Congratulations, Zivah. I'm glad you're the one that took out The Ghost." Pat replied.

Meanwhile, the *Sayeret Makal* commandos were taking intense AK-47 and Yasin RPG fire from local PLF and Hamas combatants on the rooftops. The commandos raked the roofs with the Negev machinegun and 5.56-millimeter Galil short assault rifles. Two commandos and two dozen Palestinian combatants were killed in the firefight before it ended.

Pat and Zivah ran over to Ari and Sarah. "She'll never make it to the hospital," Ari yelled," as a commando medic arrived.

The medic applied a pressure bandage to her neck and said, "Help me get her to the chopper. We'll do our best to save her."

After Sarah was airlifted to a hospital in Tel Aviv, Pat announced, "Well, this Palestinian terrorist chapter is now successfully closed."

Zivah and Ari nodded in agreement. Zivah then took photos of The Ghost's corpse and sent them to Mazar with a text message updating the mission. "Okay, let's go home. It's been a long day," she announced, "and the chief wants to debrief us at 0700 hours tomorrow."

"The commandos can clean up this mess," Ari added.

"I'll send an incident report to my superiors now," Pat mentioned.

Tel Aviv

Pat and Zivah rode with Ari because their Renault was now completely shot up and out of commission. "Let's get out of the West Bank as soon as possible. It's getting dark and we would be in jeopardy taking the bypass to Jerusalem," Zivah suggested.

"Excellent idea. I'll take the highway to Ashkelon and drive up the coast."

"Sounds good," Pat said.

Although it was only about 45 miles, it seemed like a long, long journey from Hebron to Tel Aviv for the exhausted operatives. "I feel both elated about the demise of The Ghost, and saddened because of Sarah's possible mortal wound,"

Zivah stated sincerely as they approached the city.

"I do too, and I pray she'll be okay," Pat replied.

Ari added sadly, "So do I, so do I. She's a fine partner." He then dropped Pat and Zivah off at the Hilton Tel Aviv. The lovers ate a light dinner in their hotel room. Then they cuddled up and immediately fell sound asleep.

~~~

Pat, Zivah, Ari, Fatin, and André were in attendance when Division Chief Ariel Mazar opened the debriefing meeting at Mossad Headquarters the next day.

"In recognition for the completion of a successful dangerous mission, I'm awarding Commendations of Courage to Agents Benjamin, O'Leary, Jacobi, and Keats. I will send complete mission reports to your home agencies after the debriefing." As Mazar passed out the awards, she continued, "I'll give Agent Keats her certificate when she's out of intensive care." Holding up a gold medal, she added, "I will also present her with this Medal of Valor in recognition of being wounded in battle."

Everyone applauded. Then Pat asked, "How *is* Sarah doing?"

Zivah added, "Will she make it? What is her status?"

"She's still critical, but the doctors believe she will survive. Although, Agent Keats will be sent back to the U.K. when she can travel. That's it for now. I promise to keep you updated on her condition, and will let you know when she can have visitors." Holding her hand up to prevent more questions, Chief Mazar continued, "Now, the debriefing. Let's start with Agent Benjamin."

Pat mused, *Mazar is certainly is a strong-willed and*

controlling woman. I wonder if she's bucking for Director?

The intense mission debriefing session concluded at 1400 hours. As the operatives left the conference room, Zivah asked the others, "Shall we celebrate with a nice supper?"

Everyone agreed, and Fatin added, "I should freshen up and change clothes first."

"Good idea. Let's meet down in the lobby at 1500 hours. We'll take a Mossad limo to the America House rooftop restaurant on Shaul Hamelekh Boulevard. It's the only continental kosher restaurant in Tel Aviv, and they serve very good food," Zivah suggested.

An hour later, Zivah and Fatin walked up to the male agents waiting in the lobby. The men eyed the two sensuously pleasing women attired in revealing evening dresses and high heels. While looking them up and down approvingly, Pat exclaimed, "Wow! You two are knockouts!" He put his arm around Zivah's tiny waist and ushered her toward the door.

"I certainly approve. Here, take my arm, Fatin," Ari added.

"Sorry you will be solo tonight, André," Ari said.

Pat offered, "Ditto, André."

"Us also," Zivah and Fatib chimed in.

André smiled while winking knowingly at the two couples, and with a thick French accent said, "*Bon, bon,* my friends. The evening looks very promising for you!"

Chapter Four: Gaza Strip

Flying at 5,000 feet in the nearly silent and almost invisible UH-60 Blackhawk helicopter, the team could see the moonlit Mediterranean Sea and the dune-covered coastal plain as they crossed into the Palestinian Gaza Strip territory between the southern Israeli towns of Erez and Nir'am. Pat and Ari were attired in soiled Arab *dejellabas* and black and white PLO-color *keffiyehs*. The men had beard stubbles, and Ari carried a mini Geiger counter on his belt. Zivah wore jeans with a dark turtleneck blouse, and a black full-length Arab *abaya* was stowed in her waistband pouch. All three operatives packed Berettas, wore Kevlar ballistic T-shirts, and Jordanian-made desert sandals. Their parachutes were strapped on. In her pouch, Zivah also carried a package of C4 explosive with a radio-controlled detonator that could be activated with her BlackBerry.

"The towns are dark except for a few lights in Gaza City, and there's no observable activity in the desert," Zivah advised while scanning the area with infrared binoculars.

"Most of northern Gaza looks like a huge metropolis," Pat stated.

"It pretty much is, aside from some scattered farmlands and desert areas," Zivah acknowledged. "The city of Gaza has been inhabited for 5,000 years, but the southern part of the Gaza Strip is still mostly arid desert."

They were just northeast of Beit Hanun when the green jump light came on. "It looks like a go. I'm up first," Ari announced as he opened the door of the helicopter and prepared to jump. "I'll see you two this evening, *Adonai* willing."

Pat and Zivah watched him skydive, and then open his parachute at 500 feet. They lost sight of him as the ultra-quiet helicopter sped toward Al Qubban. A few minutes later, as they flew over the Jabalyah Refugee Camp, they received a text message from Ari, *boots on ground. all peaceful. asp.*

The green light went on again as they approached Al Qubban. "Well, I'm next. See you later, Dear," Zivah said as she threw Pat a kiss.

"Tonight it is," he responded as he patted her buttocks. He watched her free-fall, and then open her chute a few seconds later. The Blackhawk headed toward the Mediterranean as Zivah disappeared in the darkness of the night.

Pat soon received a text from Zivah, *boots on ground. a ok. cobra.*

The helicopter headed out to sea for about a thousand yards, followed the coastline northward, and made an abrupt right turn to head for the shore. The green light came on and Pat scanned the shoreline highway for patrols with his infrared binoculars. Then he jumped out over the narrow Gaza City beach.

Tel Aviv

Ariel Mazar opened the meeting at 0700 hours the previous day. "Before we get started, I have an update on Agent Keats' condition. She is stable but still in intensive care. However, the doctors believe she will have a full recovery in a week or two."

Everyone in the room cheered for their wounded colleague.

"Now, down to business. Our next vital mission is

finding a dirty bomb in the Gaza Strip. Intel leads us to believe one of the Hamas lieutenants, Marzug al-Masri, is in possession of the radioactive device. Some of you know al-Masri is called The Egyptian, and he was observed in the Gaza City *souk* yesterday. Intel also suggests the dirty bomb was built in Iran and transported into Gaza from Egypt's Sinai Peninsula via a tunnel underneath the southern frontier. Moreover, the Egyptian Muslim Brotherhood may have been involved, because Hamas is an off-shoot of that organization."

"My specialty is nuclear weapons, including dirty bombs and missile warheads. So, this *is* my area of expertise." Ari offered.

"I'm well aware of your expertise, and that's why The Prussian and I selected Team Two for this mission, Agent Jacobi! Remember, I'*m* in charge of this division."

"Yes, Chief," Ari replied submissively.

There she goes again, throwing her weight around, Pat contemplated.

"As you know, Iran supports and supplies arms to Hamas. Our intel suggests Iran might have asked Hamas to test their dirty bomb in a highly populated area of Israel, such as Tel Aviv." Mazar nodded at Ari and said, "Agent Jacobi, now you can give the group a very brief description of a dirty bomb."

"Of course, Chief. A dirty bomb combines conventional explosives, such as TNT, with mildly radioactive material, such as plutonium-236 or cobalt-60. The radioactive materials can be obtained from nuclear reactors and from the black market. This type of weapon is called a 'dirty bomb' because it might provide enough radioactivity when detonated to cause some localized radioactive illness."

"There could also be significant damage caused by the conventional explosion. However, they are *not* nuclear bombs," interjected Mazar.

Ari finished his presentation with, "Detonation is the main problem, because it more than likely would be a suicide mission."

"That may not a problem for some terrorists groups, because they occasionally use women and children as suicide bombers," Zivah offered.

"Thank you for the overview, Agent Jacobi," Mazar stated as she took over the meeting. "Intel makes us confident the Iranian and Hamas leaders want to determine how many civilians will be killed in a dirty bomb explosion. What the psychological impact will be after detonation in a large city. How much mass panic and terror will it cause. How much time and expense it will take to decontaminate radiation victims. So, now you know how important this mission is.

"With Agent Keats hospitalized, and returning to London when she's able to travel, I'm assigning Team One to assist you, Agent Jacobi. You worked well together in Iran, and I expect the three of you will successfully complete this extremely vital mission ... just as you did with The Persian Caper.

"The only weapons you will take are your 9-millimeter Berettas with extra ammo because of their concealability. Other weapons can be procured from your local contacts. You will dress like Arabs, talk like Arabs, act like Arabs, smell like Arabs, and nod your heads to the right side like Arabs. If you don't, you *will* be captured, tortured, and beheaded."

"We understand, Chief," Pat interjected.

"Okay then. Insertions will be via low altitude semi-halo type jumps at 5,000 feet from a stealth helicopter, and you will deploy your parachutes at 500 feet. There's a half moon tonight, and that should provide enough light for safe landings in the flat to rolling sands and farmlands of the Gaza. Agent Jacobi is the team leader, and he will be inserted in the small desert area northeast of Gaza City near Beit Hanun. Agent Benjamin will be inserted in the farmlands south of Gaza City near Al Qubban. Agent O'Leary won't blend very well with the Arabs because of his European skin color, plus he has a slight western accent when he speaks Arabic, so he will be inserted on the beach north of Gaza Port, which is very close to central Gaza City. Of course, this is the most dangerous insertion because of constant patrols along the shoreline highway. Moreover, Gaza is the largest city in the Palestinian territories, with a population of nearly a half-million Arabs, so he *will* be at risk.

"We are inserting you in separate areas because we don't want all three of you caught at once if something goes wrong. The insertions will start at 0300 hours tomorrow, and you will meet at a safe house in Gaza City no later than that evening.

"Agent Jacobi's alias is Ibrahim Kanaan. Agent Benjamin's alias is Rafa Naser. Agent O'Leary's alias is Dani Haik. Use these names only with your contacts."

Handing out envelopes to the mission operatives, Mazar continued, "These contain forged Palestinian Authority ID cards, the safe house address with maps and directions from your insertion points, and 35,000 shekels. I've sent the name and photo of your local contact, as well as the safe house GPS coordinates, to your BlackBerrys. Your Muslim contact, Mohamed X, is anti-Hamas and a Fatah supporter. He will be waiting for you at the safe house. It's imperative that each of you give him 350 shekels when you arrive. This is important because he will then provide you with the latest info on where The Egyptian was last seen. The rest of the money is for weapons, your expenses' and payments to informants. Remember; you are accountable for every single shekel!"

The three operatives nodded in assent.

"As before, use only your code names in your BlackBerry text messages, and include me in *all* transmittals. Remember, no voice calls because the Palestinians may monitor them!

"Another very important item. You know Hamas rained a thousand Palestinian-made Qassam and Iranian-made Faji-5 rockets on Tel Aviv, New Jerusalem, and many southern Israeli towns near the Gaza recently. Several of our civilians were killed during that blitz. Of course, we retaliated by taking out the Hamas leader with a drone and destroying most of their launch sites in the Gaza. Even though a cease-fire agreement was reached, our intel indicates Hamas may have plans for something much, much bigger. So, keep your eyes and ears open for more info on their plans."

"We will, Chief, we will," Ari replied.

"Perhaps their rocket attack was an exercise to prepare Hamas for aiding Iran in air attacks on Israel, *if* Israel decides to take out Iran's nuclear research and development sites, either unilaterally or with a coalition as recommended in The Persian Caper debriefing," Pat offered.

"You may be correct, Agent O'Leary. That's for you three to find out." Mazar added, "Personally, I wonder how much of the $20.6 million dollars the U.S. President recently gave Hamas for the so-called humanitarian aid *really* went toward building rockets to attack Israel."

"That's enough conjecture for now. I'll let you know when you will be in harm's way, *if* Hamas commences more rocket attacks on Israel and IDF retaliates again by air, or with a ground invasion of the Gaza. Well, that's it. Go get that *jihadist*, The Egyptian, and destroy the damned dirty bomb in *his* territory. May *Adonai* speed you, and good hunting!"

Al Qubban

Zivah had landed so hard on the clay-mineral soil of a cabbage field that her sandaled feet ached. She was in the middle of the farmlands, and quickly buried her parachute and skydiving goggles under a huge cabbage plant. After sending the team a text message, she donned her *abaya*.

While limping toward a nearby-darkened farmhouse, a dog started barking. The elderly farmer came out of the house armed with an old 12-guage double-barreled Spanish-made Grulla shotgun. He surveyed his crops with a bright flashlight. Spotting Zivah, the Palestinian yelled in Arabic, "I thought my dog was barking at hyenas. The beasts eat my chickens. What are you doing in my field, Madame? Are you stealing my cabbage?"

Zivah replied in flawless Arabic, "I am not stealing your cabbage, kind sir. I am walking from Al Bureij to the Great Mosque in Gaza. I must be there for the first *namez* today. I crossed your farmland because I am very tired and my feet are sore from such a long journey."

"You are a good pilgrim, but I cannot help you with your journey as I must tend my fields and guard my chickens. You can stop the autobus to Gaza on the highway in that direction." The Palestinian pointed westward and continued, "It is about a half hour walk."

"Praises to Allah, kind sir," Zivah replied as she departed. After reaching the highway, she sat down on a large rock and rubbed her tender feet while waiting for arrival of the northbound bus.

A Hamas security vehicle heading north with headlights off stopped in front of Zivah a short time later. The passenger in the front seat inquired, "What are you doing sitting here in the dark, woman?"

"I am waiting for the autobus to take me to the Great Mosque in Gaza, kind sir," Zivah replied.

"You can not be out here in the night by yourself. You must have a male family member with you. Give me your papers woman."

"Of course, kind sir," Zivah responded politely as she stood and walked to the vehicle. She handed her forged Palestinian Authority identification card through the window and he viewed it with a flashlight. Meanwhile, she slipped her hands under the *abaya,* attached a silencer to her 9-millimeter Beretta, and took the safety off the weapon.

Shining the light on Zivah's face, the man commanded gruffly, "There is something wrong with this identification woman! Get in the vehicle so we can take you to headquarters."

"But, I will miss the first *namez* at the mosque, kind sir," Zivah complained with a smile. Then she swiftly pulled the Beretta from the folds of her *abaya* and shot the unsuspecting driver and passenger with one round apiece in their foreheads. Both men immediately slumped over from the lethal cranium shots. While dragging the bodies into a tomato field, she muttered, "Now I won't have to wait for the damned bus." She removed her *abaya,* then took a black and white *keffiyeh* from one of the men and wrapped it around her head to resemble a male Hamas member. Before leaving the scene, Zivah sent a text message to the team about the incident, *took out security patrol. have vehicle. cobra.*

Driving toward Gaza City, she met two oncoming Hamas security vehicles. The Palestinians in both vehicles waved at her, and she waved back. *I guess my disguise is working.*

The operative encountered a Hamas checkpoint at the southern outskirts of the city. *Now, I'll really find out if my pretext works when I stop. I hope I don't make a language error while speaking Arabic.*

She started to brake at the checkpoint when one guard eyed her suspiciously and held up his hand to stop her. However, the other guard stepped aside and motioned for her to go through. Zivah waved at them through the open window, with her arm partially hiding her face. She decided not to say anything because they might realize her voice wasn't masculine. *Whew! That was close. I guess they haven't found the bodies yet. Thank you Adonai. I've had enough excitement tonight.*

A short while later, Zivah pulled to the side of the street to get her GPS bearings. Then she sent the team a text message, *open safe house yard gate in 10 to conceal vehicle. cobra.* Not receiving a reply, she murmured, "Well, I guess I'm on my own for now."

Zivah then headed directly toward the safe house. She drove past the Palestinian Stadium and the Gaza Theater in the Zeitoun District. As she went by the Arts and Crafts Village, the morning call to prayer aired from minaret loudspeakers at two neighborhood mosques, one on each side of her. "Now that surround-sound gives me an eerie, spine-chilling feeling as a non-Muslim in enemy territory," she whispered.

Approaching the safe house, she drove around the area for a few minutes to make sure she wasn't being followed. The gate was closed, but unlocked when she finally arrived at the safe house. Zivah parked the Hamas vehicle behind the tall wall. She removed the *keffiyeh*, put her *abaya* back on, and locked the gate. Then she entered the house and announced, "*As salam' aklakoom*. I am Rafa Naser. Are you Mohamed, and has anyone else arrived?"

"I am Mohamed X. You are the first one to arrive, Madame."

Zivah gave the contact 350 shekels and declared, "I need a hot bath." Then she sent the team and Mazar a text message, *arrived. cobra.* Of course, her Beretta was within easy reach as she bathed.

Beit Hanun

The rushing desert air felt warm on Ari's face as he skydived toward two low sand dunes glimmering in the moonlight just east of the Beit Hanun. He felt a sudden jerk when he pulled the ripcord and the chute opened. The soft sand between the dunes absorbed the shock of landing on his sandaled feet. He immediately buried his parachute and skydiving goggles in the sand. Several minutes after sending his text message to the team, Ari received texts from Zivah and Pat indicating they also landed safely.

The operative approached Beit Hanun cautiously in the moonlit desert. Nearing the town, he walked along a camel trail paralleling the four-lane divided Ashqelon-Gaza Highway. An occasional Hamas patrol vehicle traveled down the highway with lights off so they wouldn't be targets for nighttime Israeli drones. When he heard them approaching, Ari crouched down on the trail to blend in with the desert sands.

That vehicle is slowing down. Maybe they spotted me, Ari contemplated as a darkened vehicle approached. He hit the ground, and readied his Beretta for a confrontation when the vehicle stopped on the shoulder of the highway 100 feet from him.

The two Palestinian occupants scanned the desert around

Ari with a spotlight. After a few minutes, one of them said in Arabic, "It must have been a hyena or a jackal. Let us leave now."

"Okay, Marzug," the other one replied.

As they pulled away, Ari wondered, *Could that have been Marzug al-Masri, The Egyptian?* He sent the incident details and his thoughts to the team, and then continued his moonlit trek toward the town.

The camel trail went under a highway overpass and toward the Beit Hanun town center. Ari stopped as he entered the long overpass tunnel so his eyes would become accustomed to the complete darkness. He suddenly focused on a pair of large green eyes glowing in the dark, spaced about six inches apart! Then he heard a low hostile growl. *Oh, oh, a leopard,* he thought while drawing his Beretta. *If it attacks, I'll have to shoot and the echo from the tunnel will waken the entire town. Maybe I should use my knife. No, that won't work when I can't see the animal in the dark."* Ari then stood tall, raised his arms to appear larger, and let out a loud growl to try to frighten the beast. The 90-pound Arabian leopard ran out the other end of the tunnel, leaving its meal of dead hare behind. Ari worried as he walked through the pitch-black tunnel, *All I need now is for a Deathstalker scorpion to sting my bare toes!*

A *muezzin's* pious call to prayer emitted from the minaret of the Um al-Nasir mosque in Beit Hanun as Ari walked past it at daybreak. After saying the first of the five daily *namez* while facing Mecca on small prayer rugs, the bazaar merchants began to open their shops and display goods for sale. Ari observed the glittering gold chains, intricate designs in the polished copper trays, and burlap sacks overflowing with aromatic Middle Eastern herbs and spices. The operative then spotted a Palestinian deliveryman unloading Gazan wool carpets from his van, so he approached the man and asked, in fluent Arabic, "Sir, are you going to Gaza City when you finish?"

"Yes, why do you ask?" was the terse response.

"I will help you unload your carpets as well as pay you, if you will give me a ride to the city."

"Help me unload and pay me 35 Israeli shekels. Then I will take you to the Gaza *souk*," the deliveryman replied.

The drive to the Old City atop a hill in central Gaza was uneventful. Several Hamas security vehicles passed them in both directions on the highway, but paid little attention to the recognizable van. The driver remained silent during the thirty-minute trip, and Ari thought, *It's good he doesn't want to talk, because I could make a mistake while speaking Arabic and he might report me to the Hamas police.* They entered the Old City through the Gate of Hebron and went past the Great Mosque of Gaza, then directly into the *souk* in the Muslim Quarter. Stopping in front of a carpet weaver's shop, the driver finally spoke to Ari. "We are here. Give me my shekels and get out of the machine."

Ari paid the Palestinian and said, "Thank you kind sir. May Allah be with your." Then he considered, *He sure didn't like me! Maybe he knows I'm not Arab, or at least not a Gazan,* as he exited the van.

Ari stood in wisps of smoke next to a street vendor cooking lamb kabobs over red-hot coals at the entrance to the bazaar. *My clothing will pick up the aroma of grilled lamb, and I'll blend in with the Palestinians better if I smell like an Arab.* He then bought a skewer of the meat for his breakfast.

Ari cautiously walked out of the Muslim Quarter,

looking over his shoulder frequently. *If I can make it to the Christian Quarter, Khalil will help me get to the safe house. He was a trustworthy contact during my last mission in Gaza, and he's also a good Christian.*

So he wouldn't attract attention, Ari casually strolled south to the Church of Saint Porphyrius in the Christian Quarter. He looked around frequently to make sure no one was following him and then entered the church. The operative exited through a side door and went into the huge garden and cemetery. *I should be secure behind these twelve-foot walls,* he deliberated.

"Is that you, Ari?" a hidden voice asked.

"It is if you are Khalil," Ari kidded his former mission contact.

Khalil ran out from behind a bush he was trimming and gave Ari a hug and a kiss on both cheeks. "Nice to see you again. What brings you back to Gaza?"

"My friend, you know I can't tell you why I'm here. But, I *can* tell you I need help getting to a safe house. There are too many Arabs on the streets and I might attract attention by walking."

"I still have my old Volkswagen beetle, and I can drive you there. But first, I must ask the priest if I can leave in the middle of my gardening."

The two friends drove out of the church garden's rear gate a few minutes later. "Let's drive around for awhile to make sure we're not being followed," Ari suggested.

Using his GPS a half hour later, Ari directed Khalil to the safe house and his Palestinian comrade dropped him off. After entering the building, Ari announced, *"As salam' aklakoom,* Mohamed. I am Abrahim Kanaan, and I have 350

Israeli shekels for you. Where is Rafa Naser?"

"She is bathing, sir."

Ari then sent a text message to Pat and Chief Mazar, *made it. asp.*

Gaza City

Pat could see the Beach Camp Palestinian refugee site to the north as he neared the ground. He landed softly on the thin strip of golden sand beach between the sea and a throng of shabby beach vendor shacks and tents lining the seafront boulevard. The operative quickly buried his chute and goggles deep in the sand above the high tide mark. Then he sent a text message to the team, *boots on ground. all quiet on western front. viper.*

Following the GPS directions, Pat walked south along the beach to avoid being spotted by Hamas security forces driving on the seafront road. *The chief was right, this certainly is a dangerous insertion,* he contemplated. The operative went past the burned-out United Nations Beach Club destroyed by Islamic extremists sometime ago. He then passed by the Grand Palace Hotel and the French Cultural Center across the boulevard.

As Pat neared the fishing fleet moored at Gaza Port, a street vendor offered *shatta* for sale. He bought a plate full of the baked crab stuffed with hot chili peppers and ate the Gazan delicacy for his breakfast. As he consumed the tasty dish, he thought, *This sure is spicy, but I'd better not show him it's too hot for me this early in the morning.* Pat just smiled, smacked his lips, and nodded his head to the right. The Arab vendor returned the smile, showing his broken yellow teeth as he puffed and coughed on a foul-smelling Egyptian cigarette.

The GPS subsequently directed Pat away from the shoreline and toward the center of the city. As he was walking through the Rimal District, the operative paused when the first daily call to prayer emitted from the Great al-Oman Mosque. *Oh, oh, I'd better take cover so the Arabs won't wonder why I'm not kneeling in prayer facing toward Mecca. Please help me God.*

He quickly stepped into the shadows of the Gaza Museum of Archeology entrance. Then a security guard noticed Pat and invited him inside. "There will be a Hamas extremist demonstration on the street as soon as the prayers are over. You may seek refuge in here, sir," he offered in Palestinian Arabic. "I am Wadid, a devout Christian Arab. I despise Hamas and do not approve of their constant demonstrations or the way they rule Gaza."

"Thank you, kind sir. I will accept your offer as I am also a Christian Arab, and my name is Dani," Pat responded in his best Arabic tongue.

"You speak with a strange accent, Dani. Where are you from?"

"I am of mixed blood, and I migrated from the United Kingdom to help with the plight of impoverished Palestinians in Gaza. However, I do not know if I can be of help *because* of the way Hamas rules the Gazans," Pat replied.

"I understand. The museum is closed now, so I can give you a private tour of the thousands of artifacts while the fools demonstrate in the street outside," the guard proposed.

"Thank you. I will pass the time with you while you show me the museum, as I have not seen it before."

"Do you know that the City of Gaza was once on an ancient trade route, and it is mentioned in the Book of Judges?" Wadid inquired.

"I do know that. I am very familiar with the Old Testament and I remember well the story of Samson and Delilah at Gaza in Judges Chapter 16. However, I do appreciate your information," Pat said courteously.

"So, you also know that Gaza was one of the Philistine strongholds mentioned in the Old Testament."

"Yes, I do."

"Good! I see that you are a learned man and we can have some interesting discussions," Wadid responded with a grin. "Here is something you may not know. The Great Mosque of Gaza was converted to the Cathedral of Saint John by the Crusaders, and then eventually reconverted back to a mosque when Saladin defeated the Crusaders."

"I did not know that, and I thank you for informing me."

Walking into a separate museum section, Wadid continued his guided tour. "Dani, here are remnants of the temple of the Philistine god Dagon, as well as some interesting images of ancient Roman and Greek gods."

Viewing a full-breasted statue of Aphrodite covered in a flimsy see-through gown, Pat inquired, "Why has Hamas not objected to this statue? It displays a desirous, life-like female figure that is nude from the waist up?"

"Only Hamas can answer that question. However, I can tell you that many Palestinian men, wearing the black and white headdress once popular with the PLO and now Hamas militants, spend a lot of time staring at the statue. I suspect some may even touch it, because the gown is frequently soiled over the sensual breasts!"

"I see. Listen! I hear shouting and gunshots outside. Is it a riot?" Pat asked.

"The Hamas demonstrators are being confronted by

Fatah supporters and there are altercations in the streets. It is not uncommon. You may as well eat and visit with me until they disperse. My wife made some very tasty *hummus* to go with my midday flatbread, olives, and tea."

"Thank you, Wadid. It will please me to dine with you," Pat replied. Then he sent a text message to the team and Mazar informing them of the incident, *refuge in museum. hamas demonstrations outside. delay in reaching safe house. viper.*

Pat enjoyed the lunch and conversation. The guard described the financial and religious plight of his family. Wadid also confided, "I pray daily for Hamas and the other Palestinian militant organizations to stop attacking Israel. Peace is the only way we can become the State of Palestine."

"I agree, sir, and I will also pray for that event. It appears Palestinian terrorists are only interested in destroying Israel *before* they seek statehood. Although, I am sure that does not hold true for the average Palestinians."

Wadid nodded in agreement. Then the streets became quiet. Pat thanked his newfound friend and left the museum.

He walked by the elegant but small and bustling Gaza Mall in the Rimal District, and then past the Half Dome of the Rock edifice. After skirting around the Old City hill, he found the safe house and reflected, *Thank you, God, for getting me here safely.* Entering the dwelling, he announced, "I am Dani Haik." He then gave Mohamed 350 shekels and inquired, "Where are Rafa and Ibrahim?"

"They are eating in the next room, sir."

Pat greeted his comrades-in-arms with hugs and gave Zivah a long, loving kiss. With a big smile on his face, Ari sent a text message to Chief Mazar, *entire team on location. asp.*

She responded immediately, *decide on plan & inform me*

asap. bushmaster.

The operatives related their adventures since arriving in Gaza. Then Pat asked Mohamed, "Can we obtain submachine guns?"

"I only have one Russian-made AK-47 full-automatic assault rifle. It is 7.62-millimeter and I have 500 rounds of ammunition."

"How much do you want?" asked Ari.

"150 Israeli shekels, sir."

Ari handed Mohamed the money and said, "Done. Bring it to us now."

When the contact returned with the weapon and ammo, Pat checked it over and announced, "It appears to be operable, although a little banged up and needs a thorough cleaning, which I'll take care of. I think it's worth the $525 U.S."

"Okay. Next on the agenda. Mohamed, where is The Egyptian now, and do you know where he is hiding the dirty bomb?" Ari asked.

"I know he was in Beit Hanun last night."

"Yes, I knew that was him on the highway as I walked to the town last night. Where is he *right now*, Mohamed?"

"I do not know about right now, but my intel leads me to believe he will be at a woman's house near the *souk* tonight, and he may be there until morning."

"Okay, you can take us there at dusk. Now, what about the bomb?" Ari asked impatiently.

"I believe it is stored somewhere in the south, but I am sorry I was not able to find out where."

"Well, that's it. So much for $300 worth of information," Pat replied with a frown.

"We should tail al-Mazri when he leaves his consort's house and hope he leads us to the dirty bomb," Zivah recommended.

"Sounds like a plan," Ari agreed.

"I do know his family is south of here at Khan Yunis," Mohamed interjected.

"He certainly wouldn't store the dangerous device near his family," Pat advised.

"Okay, then. Mohamed, we need your cell phone number so we can contact you to see if you have more intel for us." Handing Mohamed the team's cell numbers, Ari continued, "We will use text messages only. No voice calls. Can you text in English?"

"Yes, I can sir. Here is my cell number."

"I'll let the chief know our plans," Ari declared as he sent Mazar a text message.

When the orange-hued sun dipped into the Mediterranean Sea in the west, Mohamed directed the operatives to a teahouse across the street from The Egyptian's expected destination. Zivah parked the stolen Hamas security vehicle in an alley near the teahouse where they could observe the abode's entrance. Then they sat at an outdoor table in front of the café and Mohamed ordered tea, oranges, and *baklawa* for the group. The four of them sipped the hot tea and ate their evening meal while observing the consort's home as they waited for Marzug al-Masri to appear.

"This pastry is as good as Turkish *baklava* that I've always enjoyed," Pat mentioned.

"Yes, you once alleged, 'Ah! Food for a God!'" Zivah added.

"I did, on our flight from Istanbul to Lake Van during The Persian Caper. That seems like eons ago."

"*Baklawa* has the same ingredients as *baklava*, with ground pistachios, walnuts, and honey between thin layers of phyllo dough," Mohamed informed them. "Baklawa is probably just the Arabic pronunciation."

"Okay, back to business. Maybe The Egyptian is already inside," Ari suggested.

"He does not arrive before nightfall," Mohamed informed the team.

"Look! Look! I think that's him going into his consort's house. The man looks like the photo Mazar sent to our BlackBerrys," Zivah whispered excitedly.

"Yes, Madame. That is Marzug al-Masari," Mohamed agreed. As he stood up, he continued, "My job is done for now, so I will leave. I will text you if I find out where the bomb is located. *Maa salama.*"

The three operatives nodded at the Arabic goodbye as Mohamed disappeared into the darkness of the night.

"Okay, let's get comfortable in the vehicle. It may be a very long night. You two can have the back seat and I'll take the first watch," Ari volunteered. "I'll text the Chief."

Pat and Zivah curled up together on the back seat of the security vehicle and fell fast asleep. Ari woke Pat at 2400 hours and informed him, "Your turn to surveil. There's been no movement across the street, so he's still inside. Wake

Zivah for her watch at 0400 hours."

"Okay, my friend, get a good night's sleep," Pat replied as he got into the front seat next to Ari. "Tomorrow may be another long day."

Pat woke Zivah at 0400 and they traded places. "No activity since we started the stakeout."

"Got it," she responded sleepy-eyed. At dawn, the Great Mosque broadcasted the call to prayer. Zivah shook her two comrades-in-arms. "Wake up, The Egyptian is on the move. He just exited his consort's abode and he's walking toward the bazaar. Look, he's getting into a pale green Mercedes. Let's go guys!"

Deir Al-Balah

Marzug al-Masri headed south and the operatives followed at a safe distance behind him because the streets were almost empty. "Looks like he's leaving the city. Here, help me put this damned *keffiyah* on before we reach the Hamas checkpoint," Zivah requested of Pat.

Approaching the checkpoint, they observed the guards wave The Egyptian on through. "Zivah, roll down your window and point at his vehicle as we pull up." Pat recommended. "Maybe the guards will think we're escorting him because we're in a Hamas security vehicle."

"Okay, here we go!" Zivah replied. She waved at the guards and pointed at the Mercedes. The guards then waved her on through the checkpoint. Zivah whispered, Dimwits!

"Now, that was a great idea," complimented Ari.

Al-Masari accessed the Gaza-Rafah Highway and proceeded southbound. Traffic was moderate, so Zivah followed about a half mile behind him. However, the traffic was much heavier as they neared Deir al-Balah. "We'd better get a little closer in case he turns into the town, or we may lose him in the congestion," Zivah advised.

"Go ahead, you're doing a great job tailing him," Ari commented.

Pat nodded in agreement.

"We're only about half way to Khan Yunis, but it looks like he's turning off into this town," Zivah said.

"Maybe he has another consort there," Pat replied with a grin.

"He may also have official Hamas business there," Ari added. "Don't lose him now. This *could* be where he stored the dirty bomb. Be careful, the entire population of this town is Muslim. I'd better update the Chief."

They followed the Hamas lieutenant through the center of town and toward the coast. "Look, he's stopping at that fish monger's stand. Maybe he's just getting dinner for his family," Zivah commented as she pulled off the road and parked in back of a delivery truck so al-Masari wouldn't see them. A few minutes later, they watched the proprietor wrap several whole fresh fish in newspapers. Their prey put the fish in the trunk of the Mercedes, turned his vehicle around, and headed back toward the Gaza-Rafah Highway.

"Well, no bomb here," said Pat as their quarry drove south on the highway.

Khan Yunis

Nearing Khan Yunis, Ari offered, "This is the second largest urban area in the Gaza Strip. It's also the present-day stronghold of Hamas."

"And this is where Hamas launched the Qassam rockets

at Sderot that killed my dear friends a few years ago. Before that, Islamic militants killed an eight-month pregnant Israeli and her four young daughters. Then they attacked their memorial service," Zivah added. "So, we are very much in jeopardy here."

"I agree." Ari said. "During the past several years, over 2,000 Qassam rockets and mortar shells were launched at Israel from right here."

The Egyptian turned off the highway at the second exit and drove west toward the Mediterranean Sea. Prey and predator went past the medieval Khan Yunis Caravansary, and then past the huge open-air Bedouin *souk*. "Remember what Ariel Mazar said, 'Dress like Arabs, talk like Arabs, act like Arabs, smell like Arabs, and nod your heads to the right side like Arabs,'" Zivah cautioned.

Al-Masari was waved on through a checkpoint as he entered the main part of the huge city. "Same ploy, Zivah. I pray to *Adonai* it works again." stated Ari.

"You and I have beard stubbles, Ari, so we may blend in more easily. However. Zivah doesn't. Wrap your *keffiyeh* up on your chin, Zivah," suggested Pat.

"Will do. Here we go." Zivah waved at the guards and pointed at The Egyptian's Mercedes. Again, the guards waved her on through the checkpoint.

"I'll say it for you, Zivah. Dimwits," Pat whispered with a big smile.

They followed The Egyptian down the Avenue of the Eucalyptus, through town, and toward the Mediterranean Sea. Passing by a string of camels carrying camel dung for sale as fertilizer, Pat mentioned, "Now, this reminds me of Iran. The camel herders sold camel dung to fertilize Tehran's Persian gardens located behind the tall residential walls when

I lived there. Just like the Arabs do here."

"You are so right, Patrick. There may not be much cultural difference between the Iranians and the Arabs, although they are different ethnic groups," Ari suggested.

Zivah stayed several vehicles behind as she followed al-Masari. "Look. He drove into an upscale residential area near the beach. Only the affluent could afford to live here."

"This must be where he lives. Careful, we don't want him to spot us now!" Ari advised. "He's pulling in the gate of that large walled villa on the right. I can see fruit trees, flowers beds, and a pool in the courtyard."

"Well, we found his home. Now what?" Pat asked.

"Stakeout!" Ari and Zivah said in unison.

"I can park in the shadows of that eucalyptus grove and we can watch the entire compound from there." Zivah suggested.

"Good, Let's hide this Hamas vehicle before someone spots it," Ari recommended.

"We can also see the nice sandy beach from here," Pat mentioned. "There's men bathing in the sea, but no women."

"Muslim women are forbidden to bathe with swimsuits in public," Ari explained.. "It's against *shiria* law."

Zivah parked the vehicle in a strategic location for observing the villa and its entrances. Then Pat and Ari laid palm fronds and eucalyptus branches on the vehicle for concealment. "This looks good. Zivah, you text the Chief and update her while I walk down to the road and buy our dinner from the beach vendors," Ari said.

"I'll take a lamb kabob or two with flatbread and goat cheese," said Zivah as she rubbed the hunger pangs of her stomach. "Also, a yogurt drink."

"Ditto for me," Pat added. "We haven't eaten since last night and we're all hungry."

"You've got it. I'll pick up something for breakfast as well. Keep alert, and make sure the AK-47 is ready for action, Patrick."

"Will do," Pat replied. As Ari headed toward the beach, Pat asked Zivah, "Why don't we just capture The Egyptian and force him to tell us where the dirty bomb is hidden?"

"He's too smart for that, and you know we don't torture our prisoners to obtain information. So, Ari's plan to follow him is the best solution we have for now."

"Well, we're locked into doing it the hard way. *C'est la guerre*," Pat commented.

"Yes, we *are* fighting a war on terrorism."

"I'll send in a MAV to see what's going on in the villa."

"Good idea, Patrick. The Micro Aerial Vehicle is a great covert op tool, as we discovered during The Persian Caper mission in Iran."

The two operatives watched and listened to the MAV's transmissions as Pat sent the bumblebee-sized device from room to room in the villa. "All I can see and hear is family activity. Nothing about the dirty bomb," Zivah advised Pat. "You may as well roost it in the kitchen where most of the activity is."

"Done."

Ari returned a short while later with a sack of food and said, "Here's all you asked for and more. We won't go hungry tonight or tomorrow. Enjoy!"

The operatives had just finished their evening meal when

Ari received a text message from Mohamed, *my informant believes your commodity is in tunnel near rafah. maybe the airport. mx.*

Ari read the text to his team, and then forwarded it to Mazar. "That's good news! However, we still need to follow The Egyptian to find the tunnel and destroy the dirty bomb."

Ariel then sent a message to the team, *follow him to the tunnel. Take him out & destroy the bomb. bushmaster.*

"Is she a mind reader?" Pat asked.

"No, she's just the Chief," said Ari. "Let's get some sleep. Same shifts as last night."

Rafah

Zivah woke her comrades at sunrise. "Time to get up and have a bite to eat. We have to be ready in case The Egyptian heads for Rafah. Patrick, why don't you activate the MAV. We just may pick up *some* intel." The operatives were nibbling on persimmons, pomegranates, big sweet and juicy strawberries, and sipping bottled water when al-Masari drove the Mercedes out of his villa. "Time to go, gentlemen. He's got a male passenger now and may be on his way to Rafah. Hurry, Patrick. Retrieve the MAV."

"I'll text the Chief," said Ari. "Patrick, double-check the AK-47."

"It's locked, loaded, and ready to go," Pat replied.

They followed the Mercedes through town, and al-Masari entered the southbound lanes of the Gaza-Rafah Highway. "Here we go! I have a good feeling about this," Zivah exclaimed.

Chief Mazar replied to Ari's text, *sending coral & sidewinder to sufa idf base & will be available for backup.*

bushmaster.

Ari read Mazar's text to the others.

The operatives followed The Egyptian and his passenger as the highway passed through the arid desert. There were several southbound vehicles ahead of her, so she stayed behind them. "He's heading for the Rafah border crossing."

"The tunnel where the dirty bomb is stored wouldn't be right at the official frontier crossing," Ari advised. "But it must be close by."

"Looks like he's pulling off into the old Yasser Arafat International Airport," Pat said. "Is it still operational?"

"No, Patrick. It's been closed since 2002 and is pretty much destroyed," Zivah answered. "That's probably where the tunnel to the Sinai Peninsula starts."

Ari grinned and said, "I do believe you're right. Now *I* have a good feeling about this! There's hundreds of tunnels under the border from homes and tents in the town of Rafah, but not from this old airport."

"Got it," said Pat.

"If they stop, drive on by and wave at them so they won't suspect us. Hopefully, they'll believe we're merely a Hamas security patrol," suggested Ari.

"Will do," agreed Zivah.

"This makes sense. It's only about two miles from the Rafah to the Kerem Shalom crossing points. So, it would be impossible for al-Masri to dig a tunnel between the two border stations right on the frontier without being noticed by the guards," Pat rationalized.

Meanwhile, prey and predators drove past Bedouins tending camels near their black goat hair tents on the old airport grounds. The Egyptian stopped in front of the airport maintenance building past the damaged air traffic control tower. Then he and his passenger stared at the Hamas vehicle driven by Zivah. As the operatives went past the parked Mercedes, they waved at al-Masari and kept going.

"I sure hope they bought it," said Ari.

"Looks like they did," informed Zivah as she looked in the rearview mirror. "They're driving into the building now and just closed the garage door."

"That has to be where the tunnel entrance is," Pat exclaimed. "We've found it!"

"Okay. Turn around and park alongside the building," Ari said. "We'll find a way in. Patrick, double check the AR-47 again and make sure it's ready for combat. Zivah, do the same with your Beretta after you park. Patrick and I will check ours as well."

Ari sent the chief another text message, *believe tunnel starts inside maintenance building south of arafat control tower. team going in. send backup now. asp.*

Mazar responded to Ari immediately, *done. stealth helio eta 10. bushmaster.*

"Okay, Fatin and Andr are on their way. They'll be here in 10 minutes. Zivah, hurry and pick the lock on this side door."

Zivah quickly opened the door and the operatives entered the building with their weapons drawn and ready. Ari turned on his mini Geiger counter and scanned the area when he took the lead. He held his index finger to his lips as they moved forward to locate the Mercedes.

Zivah spotted the vehicle parked next to an oil change pit in the middle of the large building and pointed toward it. The

Egyptian and his passenger where not observable, so Ari motioned down the pit and under the floor toward Egypt. Pat and Zivah nodded. Approaching, he spotted a narrow entrance to the tunnel in the pit and whispered, "They're in the tunnel. Patrick, text the chief. We're going in now."

"Will do."

Dropping down into the pit, Ari added "Okay, Patrick, you take the lead now with the AK-47. No talking, hand signals only. I'll go second and scan the tunnel with the Geiger counter buzzer off so it's not heard. Zivah, you're our rear guard. We have to watch out for IEDs!"

Pat entered the dark tunnel, and then held his fist up for the team to stop. He pointed at his eyes, and then the black tunnel to indicate their eyes needed to adjust to the darkness. Ari and Zivah nodded in agreement. After one minute of eye adjustment, Pat waved them forward and slowly proceeded on the downward slope into the depths of the long tunnel.

Fatin and André were enjoying the view of the Mediterranean Sea and downtown Tel Aviv over *hummus*, celery sticks, and glasses of Sabra at the top of the Shalom Tower. The chief interrupted their quiet time when she sent them a text message, *need immediate backup for teams one and two. sending limo. helio wheels up in 20. full combat gear with ballistic vests and uzis. bushmaster.*

"It's going to be tight, so let's get going," said André.

"You're right. The Mossad limo will take us to HQ to gear up and the helio will take off from the roof."

While boarding the UH-60 Blackhawk helicopter, the operatives received another text from the chief, *asp, viper, cobra entering hamas tunnel from oil pit at arafat airport maintenance bldg south of old tower. bushmaster.* Fatin gave the pilot the landing zone location as they took off.

The stealth helicopter flew southwest and into the Negev Desert. Then it paralleled the Gaza Strip border from the Israeli side. The pilot headed due west just past Sufa. It only took seconds for the helicopter to cross the border and reach the defunct Yasser Arafat International Airport. The pilot set down near the stolen Hamas security vehicle used by Pat, Zivah, and Ari earlier.

"Okay. Here we go," said Fatin. "Safety off our Uzis, and be alert."

"*Oui, bon ami,*" replied André.

"I'll be waiting for you and the others at kibbutz Sufa IDF Base," the pilot informed them. "I can be back here in less than a few minutes."

"Good. The chief will let you know when to extract us." As the helicopter took off, the operatives entered the maintenance building and quickly found the tunnel entrance in the oil pit. "I'll take point," Fatin said. "Watch our rear, André. We can't tell who might have seen us land."

Pat led the team down the tunnel slope until it leveled off at 200 feet below the ground's surface. He pointed out well-shored walls and a strong ceiling. Then he signaled "IR" for evidence of Iranian engineers handiwork. Zivah and Ari nodded in understanding.

Ari shined a penlight at his mini Geiger counter. The meter pegged at the high end of the scale when he directed it ahead in the tunnel.

Pat immediately pointed at his ears and then in the same direction that Ari had pointed. Next, he displayed five fingers ten times.

Zivah and Ari understood that their enemies and the bomb were only 50 feet away from them.

Slowly advancing on the targets, the operatives spotted The Egyptian and his associate wearing headlamps and loading the bomb into a wheelbarrow. Pat yelled "Fire, fire," and opened up with the AK-47.

Ari yelled, "Don't hit the bomb!" as he and Zivah opened up with supporting fire from their Berettas. Both Palestinians went down without returning a shot. Covered by Pat and Zivah, Ari ran forward, "They're both dead. Good shooting." He then sent photos of the two dead Hamas combatants and the dirty bomb to the Mazar with a text message describing the incident.

As Fatin and André approached the battle scene, three Islamic Jihad young men wearing black ski masks came up from behind them and started shooting at the two operatives with Iranian-made Khaybar 5.56-millimeter full-automatic assault rifles. André took three rounds in his ballistic vest, and Fatin took four rounds in her vest. As André went down from the impact of the rounds, he yelled "Sacré Bleu, I'm hit!"

Fatin also yelled, "I'm hit!" as she went down.

Hearing the shots and yells, Pat and Ari headed up the tunnel toward Fatin and André. Zivah stayed behind to attach the C-4 plastic explosive and radio controlled detonator on the dirty bomb.

Meanwhile, André fired his Uzi on the approaching Gazans while on the ground. Pat hollered, "Stay down, stay down," as he also fired at the Islamic Jihadists with his AK-47. All three terrorists went down permanently.

Ari helped Fatin up as Pat was helping André off the ground. Zivah approached and exclaimed, "Let's go. We don't know what might be heading this way from the Egyptian side, and the dirty bomb's set to explode. I'll detonate it as soon as we're out of the tunnel."

"Great job," Ari responded. "Let's double-time out of here."

Exiting the tunnel, the five operatives hurried out of the oil pit and ran toward the side door of the old maintenance building. "I'll text the chief with an update and request our extraction," Ari announced.

André asked, "How about a Predator drone to take out any other Islamic Jihadists?"

"We will be long gone before a drone can reach us here. Zivah, set off the bomb now!"

Zivah blew up the dirty bomb by triggering it with her BlackBerry, and the operatives heard a muffled explosion from underground. "Sounds like it's done," commented Pat with a smile. "They won't be using the contaminated tunnel for quite a while."

"And the dead terrorists have conveniently disappeared," added Ari. "Good job everyone!"

A few minutes later, the ultra-quiet Blackhawk helicopter picked up the five operatives. "Man the port and starboard machineguns," the pilot ordered. "We may have company."

"Roger that. I'll take the portside," said Zivah as she manned the Negev 5.56-millimeter gun.

"And I have the starboard gun," added Pat.

"The rest of us will feed the ammo if needed," stated Ari.

As the pilot lifted off, several rifle rounds hit the

starboard side panels of the helicopter. Pat hollered, "Incoming ... but I can't identify where they're coming from."

"Just spray the perimeter on the starboard," advised Ari.

Pat opened up with the Negev and sprayed the area left to right, then right to left. The incoming rounds ceased. "That did it," exclaimed Pat.

"Excellent shooting, Patrick," commented Zivah.

"I agree," said the pilot. "You can be my gunner anytime, Agent O'Leary."

It only took the pilot a few seconds to fly across the border into Israel. Then he headed north toward Tel Aviv. While in-flight, Pat and André sent incident reports to their respective agencies.

~~~

Chapter Five: Israel

Tel Aviv

Chief Ariel Mazar opened the debriefing meeting at 0700 hours the next day. The Prussian, Pat, Zivah, Ari, Fatin, and André were in attendance. "Okay, the first item: Agent Keats is on her way to the U.K. as we speak. She will totally recover in a few weeks and soon be ready for MI6 mission assignments." Everyone in the room cheered and applauded for their wounded colleague.

"Now, down to business. Our Mossad Director has the floor."

The Prussian stood and saluted the agents. "In recognition of the successful completion of an extremely dangerous mission, I'm awarding Commendations of Courage to Agents Benjamin, O'Leary, Jacobi, Izmiri, and Chevalier." As Mazar passed out the awards, The Prussian continued, "Agents O'Leary and Chevalier have proved themselves to me and can be on my teams anytime. I will personally call your directors and tell them the very same thing. Now, I have an important announcement. Agent Chevalier is being transferred back to France. It appears the DGSE requires his experience to track down and eliminate an al-Qaeda terrorist cell in the greater Paris area." Everyone stood and applauded André Chevalier as The Prussian was leaving the conference room.

"Now, the debriefing. We'll start with team leader, Agent Jacobi," announced Mazar. The intense mission debriefing session concluded at 1600 hours. Everyone then wished André good hunting in Paris.

As the operatives left the conference room, Ari suggested, "Let's all celebrate with a few drinks and an elegant meal."

Chief Mariel Mazar then announced, "The Gaza Strip teams need some down time. Therefore, Agents Benjamin, O'Leary, Jacobi, and Ismiri will take a mandated four days off for rest and recuperation. You may check out vehicles in our motor pool if you desire. However, keep your BlackBerrys on 24-7 in case we have a critical situation and need you back ASAP. That's it ... you're free to go."

Nazareth

The next day, Zivah checked-out a new violet-colored Lamborghini Gallardo two-seat convertible from the Mossad Motor Pool at 0800 hours. She and Pat then headed north on the coast highway. When she floor-boarded the luxury sports car on a long straightaway, Pat exclaimed, "Wow, what acceleration! You *will* let me drive this beauty, won't you?"

"Perhaps, if you're nice to me, Dear."

"I'm always nice to you!"

"I know. You really should be driving, in case the Takavar commandos come after us again."

"Any time, my love, any time. Speaking of the Iranians, it was good you thought about bringing the two Uzis and extra magazines in the satchel nestled between my feet."

"You can't be too careful these days. I'll drive to my parent's home, and you can take over from there while we tour the Golan Heights and the Northern Israel Plateau." Zivah thought a moment, and then added, "I just know Mama and Papa will love you. Of course, not in the way I do. However, Papa does have a problem with your Christian faith. During my last visit, he frowned fearfully when I told him you were a devout Catholic."

"I understand. We'll just see what happens when we get there."

The two lovers were silent as they mulled over the possible consequences when Pat met Zivah's parents. The warm, gentle Mediterranean Sea breeze and tranquil Hebrew music from the radio finally relaxed them.

"Patrick, have you ever thought about converting to Judaism?"

"No, I never did. Have you ever thought about converting to Christianity, or perhaps joining Jews for Jesus to see what it's all about?"

"To be honest, I did consider looking into Jews for Jesus once, and I would like to know more about Christianity. Perhaps you can tell me about your faith during our travels."

"Of course I will. We'll have plenty of time during our four days of R and R."

Zivah turned inland at Hadera and they were soon at Alufa. They approached Nazareth a few minutes later. Driving by the Grotto of Mary, Pat said, "Let's stop here to begin your Christian lessons. This is where Mary and Joseph lived when the Angel Gabriel announced the coming of Jesus."

"See, I didn't know that, and I lived nearby during my younger years."

The next stop was Mary's Well. "Zivah, this is where The Virgin Mary drew water for her family."

She nodded in acknowledgement and continued on through town, then she suddenly cried out, "Patrick, Patrick, let's stop at this beautiful church. I've always wanted to see the interior."

"Okay. That's Saint Joseph Church. It's built over the grotto where Joseph had his carpentry shop. That's also where he taught Jesus His carpentry skills."

Kibbutz Lavi

They headed north toward Kibbutz Lavi after visiting the other Christian sites in Nazareth. The road went through Cana, where Jesus performed His first miracle, and Pat told Zivah the story of turning water into wine.

Zivah then turned into the kibbutz drive and entered the front gate. "This gate is locked at dusk to keep out 'unwanted visitors.'"

"Oh. Palestinian terrorists?"

"Yes. Now, look to your right. See the tall, barren Golan Heights with the beautiful, azure hued Sea of Galilee at their base?

"I do. What a spectacular view!"

"That grassy plain between us and the Sea of Galilee is the Horns of Hattin. That's where the Muslim Saladin and his followers defeated the Crusaders during the twelfth century."

"I remember reading about that great battle in college. Zivah, you certainly grew up in an area with lots of history, as well as magnificent beauty!"

"Do you know what Kibbutz Lavi means, Patrick?"

"Well, I know kibbutz is group. What is lavi?"

"Lion. We are a group of lions."

"I see. So you fight your enemies like lions."

Zivah just smiled. She drove past the first class hotel and parked the Lamborghini. Then they walked past the bomb shelters to her parent's home.Mama greeted them at the front door, and she and Zivah hugged and kissed each other. "Well child, introduce me to your handsome man." Zivah made the introductions, then Mama gave Pat a warm, welcoming hug and a kiss on each cheek. "Come, Papa is in the kitchen."

Papa hugged Zivah and expressed, "Welcome my little one. So, this is your Christian American gentleman. *Shalom!* Welcome to my home."

"*Shalom!* sir. I'm pleased to finally meet you." Then Pat thought, *So far, so good. Maybe they'll accept me.*

Pat and Papa chatted about life in the United States and compared the two countries. "You know, Israel is very westernized and there's not much difference between our countries, except for the kibbutz life," Pat offered.

"Do not overlook the difference between our two major religions, young man," Papa responded.

"I won't, sir. However, I firmly believe that Christianity and Judaism are very close in their beliefs. For example, we both believe in the Old Testament."

"You are correct, except for a few of the books." Papa looked intensely at Pat and then added, "However, we believe Jesus Christ was a prophet, not the son of God. So, the New Testament books are not part of our religion, and therein lies the major difference between our faiths."

The conversation continued for a while and eventually changed to a learning session about the two cultures. Mama and Zivah joined the discussion at that point. By suppertime, Pat felt that Zivah's parents were warming up to him. At least a little in Papa's case.

"It is time to go to the dining hall. Meat or dairy seating?" Mama asked Papa.

"Meat seating, to honor our distinguished American guest," Papa decided.

Zivah explained, "Patrick, meat and dairy food can't be consumed at the same tables or with the same tableware. According to our religious beliefs, if the tableware are accidentally interchanged, they must be buried in the ground for seven days before they can be used again."

Pat surmised, *Yet another difference between our religions and cultures.*

Sea Of Galilee

After their departure the next morning, Zivah suggested, "Patrick, let's go to Tiberias and see the Crusader fortress."

"Okay." Pat drove the Lamborghini down the hill toward the Sea of Galilee.

"Tiberias is where Jesus calmed the stormy waters and walked on the surface. He also performed the miracle of a plentiful catch of fish to feed His followers there," informed Pat.

"I remember hearing those stories. Like Papa said, Jesus was a prophet to us." A few minutes later she announced, "We're approaching Kibbutz Daganyya. It was founded in 1909, and captured by a Syrian tank crew during the 1973 Yom Kippur War."

Pat drove through Magdala, the home of Mary Magdalene, and then by the Mount of Beatitudes. "This is where Jesus gave the Sermon on the Mount."

Zivah nodded. "I knew about that."

He continued his story of the life of Christ as they went past Tabagha. "Now, this is where Jesus fed 5,000 of His followers with the miracle of the Multitude of Loaves and Fishes."

"Interesting."

At Capernaum, he finished his dialogue about Jesus with, "This was the center of Christ's ministry in Galilee."

"I see, thank you for the lesson, Patrick."

Golan Heights

They crossed the River Jordan on Jacob's Daughters Bridge and entered the Golan Heights region. Driving up the mountain, Zivah suggested, "We can stop at the Golani Brigade Monument and Museum, if you want."

"No, I've seen it before and was very impressed. I also remember the many 'Danger Mines' signs along the trail."

"You probably know then, this region belonged to Syria before the Yom Kippur War. We administered the region after the war until the 1980s when Israel unilaterally annexed it."

Pat replied, "Yes, I did know that. Golan Heights was still part of Syria and under Israeli administration the last time I toured the region."

"Syria keeps trying to reclaim it, and the Syrians are even capturing U.N. troops patrolling the border now."

"Imagine that! With all their internal warfare and domestic problems."

Up on the Golan Plateau, Pat sped north across the Syrian Desert on the Old Beriut Road. They went past the U.N. barracks to the east of the highway. Then by El

Quenitera, Mansura, and Mas'ada Druze villages. Damascus was a mere 35 miles due east when they went past the Damascus Road intersection.

"As friendly as the Iranians are with the Syrian regime, this would be a good place for Takavar commandos to sneak into Israel and come after us, Patrick. I have an eerie feeling, as if something bad is going to happen. I'm certainly glad *you're* driving!"

"Well. Let's test this baby out and see what she has under the hood in case we are chased by the Iranians." Pat floor boarded the Lamborghini. The high-powered sports car shot forward and was doing 150 miles-per-hour in a few seconds.

"Wow! So much for that!"

Pat slowed down and said, "We're on holiday, so let's not worry about the Iranians anymore, Dear."

"Okay, my love. Our Predator drones would probably take them out anyway."

Approaching Baniyas village, the operatives enjoyed a panoramic view of majestic snow covered Mount Hermon.

"Since we took over the Golan Heights, Israel has developed ski resorts on the southern slopes of the beautiful mountain."

"I heard about that. Let's go skiing there one of these days."

"Okay. I bet I'm a better skier than you!"

Pat just smiled.

While stopped at Baniyas Falls for a drink of the ice-cold water, Zivah informed Pat, "The falls are fed by the melting snows on Mount Hermon. This is a major source for the River Jordan, and the waters are alleged to bring eternal life to all that drink from it."

"Yes, Zivah. Remember, I've been here before? Nonetheless, let's drink a toast to eternal life for both of us."

"Of course. You realize I just wanted you to know how smart I am!"

"I do! I do! This is also where Jesus announced to the apostle Peter, 'The church will be built on this rock.' He then changed the apostle's name from Simon to Peter."

Metulla

Heading west, they left the Golan Heights region and drove by Biblical Dan. Their next stop was the Good Fence border crossing at Metulla.

The operatives went into a machine gun fortification near the crossing. "Zivah, dear Zivah. *Shalom!*" an IDF Lieutenant exclaimed as he gave her a hug and kissed both her cheeks.

Oh no, not another one of Zivah's past lovers, Pat speculated.

"Patrick, meet my cousin Zechariah."

"*Shalom!* Zechariah. Any relative of Zivah's is a friend of mine," Pat offered.

"And, any friend of Cousin Zivah's is a friend of mine! Pleased to meet you, Patrick."

The three discussed the problem of Iran-supported Hezbollah firing artillery shells at Northern Israeli settlements, and Israeli artillery units returning the fire.

"Just as it was the last time I was here." Pointing north at the mountains in Lebanon, he continued, "Except back then it was the PLO firing from that rocky mountain top."

Pat and Zivah walked over to the Good Fence gate and

110

talked to several Lebanese Christians crossing the border to work in Israel. The workers described their pitiful life while under Hezbollah control, as well as how free and welcome they felt while working in Israel.

Leaving Metulla, the operatives drove through the Hula Valley and went past Tell Hay. They stopped at the Safed artist village to stretch their legs while admiring the work of local artists.

Then they went over the Gilan Mountains. "This area reminds me of the Sierra Nevada Mountains back home," Pat remarked.

"How lovely it must be. We also have 2,000-year-old olive trees here. They are part of the largest olive grove in Israel."

Continuing west toward the Mediterranean, they arrived at Acre on the Bay of Hafia. As they drove past an ancient fortress on the waterfront, Zivah mentioned, "This was a Canaanite as well as a Phoenician port and it's 4,000-years-old now. Acre also was the capital of the Crusader Kingdom in the Holy Land during the Crusades."

Pat nodded. "I didn't know that."

Haifa

The operatives headed south toward Haifa on the Coast Highway. The sea breeze felt good on their faces after being in the hot Syrian Desert and warm Israeli inland valleys.

"Patrick, I still have that eerie feeling. I sense that someone is following us."

"I do too. Although, I keep looking behind us and haven't seen anyone suspicious. Just keep alert, and have the Uzi's ready for action."

"I'll text the chief and let her know what we suspect."

Ariel Mazar immediately replied, *watch your backs. intel informs us there may be a contingent of takavar commandos in your area. shin bet looking for them now. will keep you advised. bushmaster.*

They went on into Haifa without incident. "This city is known as 'The Gateway to the North,' Patrick." Passing by the unique Illegal Immigrant Ship Monument in the center of town, Zivah explained, "The edifice is a memorial for the 1948-1949 Jewish exoduses to Palestine. Its almost sacred for the older folks that arrived during the exodus and infiltrated past British-blockaded Palestine. They remember their voyages and unsanctioned landings in great detail. The Navy Museum is built around one of those ships."

"Yes, I observed the monument the last time I was here. It's quite extraordinary."

On the south side of town, Zivah excitedly cried out, "Patrick, Patrick, turn left at the next intersection. We can take the main highway to Mount Carmel. I'm not ready to return to the hustle of hectic Tel Aviv, and there's a wonderful resort on the slopes where we can relax and enjoy each other for the next few days."

"Sounds good to me. We're on our way!"

Mount Carmel

"Mount Carmel is called 'The Vineyard of God.' It's where Elijah hid from King Ahad, as documented in the Old Testament."

"Now, that's very informative, and something I didn't know before. Look, we can see the picturesque mountain and the deep green forest on its slopes ahead."

"Look over there, Patrick. That narrow multi-story building is part of the University of Haifa campus. That's where Chief Mazar earned her Bachelor of Arts degree before she went to Harvard for her PhD."

"I understand the university now teaches American Jewry."

"Yes it does. It's the first time the subject has been taught in Israel, Patrick."

They soon arrived at the Carmel Forest Spa Resort, located in the heart of the Carmel Forest. When the parking valet opened the doors of the Lamborghini, Pat advised him, "Just park it and keep a close eye on this violet beauty. No joy rides!"

The valet smiled wryly and said, "Yes sir!"

Pat opened the trunk for the bellhop, and Zivah handed Pat the heavy satchel containing their two Uzis and six spare magazines full of ammunition.

After checking-in, they showered to clean off the desert dust. Then the lovers viewed the sunset over the sparkling Mediterranean Sea from their private deck.

"I'm hungry, Patrick. Let's have dinner at the formal dining room. It serves exquisite continental-style kosher cuisine."

"You know, Zivah, I admire your lifestyle. Let's go dine in luxury."

After a delicious meal of cabbage stuffed with spicy ground beef and rice, accompanied with Mount Carmel white wine, Pat said, "Now, that was a great meal!"

"I'm glad you liked it. *Holishkes* is one of my favorite dishes."

"By the way, I understand Israeli and Palestinian peace talks are starting up again."

"Yes. They will ultimately reach an agreement and sign a peace pact … as they have done many times in the past. However, Palestinian terrorist groups will attack Israel the very next day, just as they have done every time a peace treaty was signed in the past."

"I surmise the *jihadists* don't want peace."

"No, they certainly don't. They just want to eliminate all Jews and thus Israel."

The two operatives strolled hand-in-hand through the lush resort gardens, guided by the moonlit evening. Automatic gunfire from the forest pierced the tranquil silence of the night just as they reached their suite and unlocked the door. Several rounds shattered the picture window next to the door.

"Inside! Take cover! It's the Iranians!" Pat yelled.

Zivah dived for the satchel and tossed an Uzi and several 40-round magazines to Pat. "I'll text the chief for immediate aid while you return fire."

"Good. Then help me keep them from advancing on us," Pat hollered over the din.

Both operatives continued to fire with their selector switches set on full automatic, as bullets whizzed past them. "I'm on my last mag, Patrick."

"My Uzi's empty. I'm switching to my Beretta," Pat responded.

"Me to."

Just then, with all the windows blown out and the walls peppered with rounds, Zivah received a text from Ariel

Mazar, *infrared surveillance drone shows 10 assailants in the forest firing at you. believed to be iranian takavar commandos. shin bet team nearby & approaching from iranians east rear flank to prevent being hit by friendly fire. they have the Iranians coordinates & can see their infrared images. bushmaster.*

Zivah relayed the information to Pat. He replied, "We're taking them out ... but now I'm on my last pistol mag," as he made a speedy tactical reload.

"Here, catch," Zivah yelled as she tossed one of her two remaining full Beretta magazines to Pat.

"Thanks. Make every shot count!"

The Shin Bet team arrived a few seconds later and the Iranians were caught in the crossfire of Mossad operatives and Shin Bet agents. The Shin Bet agents were heavily armed with IWI Tavar 5.56-millimeter bullpup full-automatic assault rifles equipped with night vision optics.

"Good timing. I just ran completely out of ammo," Pat advised Zivah.

"Me too. Whew, that was a close one! The Shin Bet agents will finish off any survivors."

A minute later, Mazar sent another text message to Zivah, *firefight over. no survivors. leader was takavar captain kadar irani. hold fire now. shin bet coming toward you. good work. bushmaster.*

When the Shin Bet agents arrived at the operatives' suite, the team leader gave Zivah a big smile, walked up to her, hugged her warmly, and kissed her on both cheeks. "My dear, sweet Zivah. *Shalom!* How are you!"

"*Shalom!* Just fine now, Philip. Thanks to you. We ran out of ammo soon after your team arrived! How in the world did Takavar commandos get into Israel?"

"Our intel indicates they entered at the Good Fence crossing disguised as Lebanese Christian workers. We'll find out for sure tomorrow."

"That's probably correct. Kadar Irani was a Hezbollah combatant for many years, and he made several sorties from Lebanon into northern Israel back then."

The Shin Bet agent nodded in agreement. Then he added, "Irani's last words were, 'Someone will get Agents O'Leary and Benjamin for killing our Vevak agents and Revolutionary Guardsmen!'"

"Well, they *will* try again. But, we'll be prepared. Philip, this is my very dear friend, Patrick."

"*Shalom!* Patrick. You are a very lucky man to be with Zivah."

"*Shalom!* Philip. How well I know." With an unshakable pensive feeling, Pat pondered, *Here we go again!!!*

War is hell.

William Tecumseh Sherman

~~~

Appendix

List Of Characters

Protagonists

Patrick O'Leary - Code Name *Viper*:

    Mossad Special Operations Team One

    Alias in Gaza: DanI Haik

    American CIA Chief Liaison Agent

    Irish/Spanish American - Catholic

Zivah (Splendor) Benjamin - Code Name *Cobra*:

    Mossad Special Operations Team One

    Alias in Gaza: Rafa Naser

    Israeli Mossad Agent

    Hebrew - Jewish

Ari (Aristotle nickname) Jacobi - Code Name *Asp*:

    Mossad Special Operations Team Two

    Alias in Gaza: Ibrahim Kanaan

    Israeli Mossad Agent

    Hebrew - Jewish

Sarah Keats - Code Name Coral:

    Mossad Special Operations Team Two

    British MI6 Agent

    Irish/Anglo - Anglican

Fatin (Alluring) Izmiri - Code Name *Coral*:

Mossad Team Special Operations Three

Israeli Mossad Agent

Turkish/Arab Palestinian

-Antiochian Orthodox Christian

André Chevalier - Code Name *Sidewinder:*

Mossad Special Operations Team Three

French DGSE Agent

French - Catholic

Ariel Mazar - Code Name *Bushmaster:*

Mossad Special Operations Division Chief

Hebrew - Jewish

The Prussian:

Mossad Director

Hebrew - Jewish

Cailin Rinesmann:

Israeli Defense Force Captain

Hebrew - Jewish

Christo Alexander:

Cypriot Cyprus Intelligence Service Agent

Greek/Cypriot. - Greek Orthodox

Halie Georgandas:

Cypriot Cyprus Intelligence Service Agent

Greek/Cypriot - Greek Orthodox

Antagonists

Major Mohammad Amir:

Iranian Takavar commando leader

Iranian - Muslim.

Abdul al-Yemeni (The Ghost):

Palestine Liberation Front (PLF) member

Yemeni/Arab Palestinian - Muslim.

Adib:

West Bank informant and double agent

Arab Palestinian - Muslim

Marzug al-Masri (The Egyptian):

Hamas lieutenant

Egyptian/Arab - Muslim.

Captain Kadar Irani:

Iranian Takavar commando leader

Past Hezbollah member

Iranian - Muslim.

Other Characters

Abdullah:

West Bank informant

Arab Palestinian - Muslim

Khalil:

Gazan contact

Arab Palestinian - Christian

Mohamed X:

Gazan contact

Arab Palestinian - Muslim

Wadid:

Gaza Museum guard

Arab Palestinian - Christian

~~~

Weapons List

Pistols

Beretta Model PX4 Storm Compact, Italian-made 9-millimeter semi-automatic pistol.

Beretta Model PX4 Storm Subcompact, Italian-made 9-millimeter semi-automatic pistol.

Beretta Model 170, Italian-made low-powered .22 Long Rifle caliber semi-automatic pistol.

Manhurin PPK, French-made .380 caliber semi-automatic pistol.

Sig Sauer Model P290RS Sub-Compact, Swiss-made 9-millimeter semi-automatic pistol.

Walther Model PPK, German-made .380 caliber semi-automatic pistol.

Assault Rifles

AK-47, Russian-made 7.62-millimeter full/semi-automatic assault rifle, 600 rounds-per-minute.

IMI Galil, Israeli-made 5.56-millimeter full-automatic short assault rifle, 650-750 rounds-per-minute.

IWI Tavar, Israeli-made 5.56-millimeter full/semi-automatic bullpup assault rifle, 750-900 rounds-per-minute.

Khaybar, Iranian-made 5.56-millimeter full/semi/ 3-round burst automatic assault rifle, 800-850 rounds-per-minute.

M-2 Carbine, American-made, .30 caliber carbine full/semi-automatic rifle, 850-900 rounds-per-minute.

Machine Guns

Skorpion, Czechoslovakian-made 9-millimeter full/semi-automatic machine pistol, 850 rounds-per-minute.

Negev, Israeli-made 5.56-millimeter full-automatic machinegun, 850-1,150 rounds-per-minute.

PP-2000, Russian-made 9-millimeter full/semi-automatic submachine gun, 600 rounds-per-minute.

Uzi, Israeli-made 9-millimeter full automatic/single shot submachine gun, 600 rounds-per-minute.

Rocket Propelled Grenade Launchers

Yasin, Palestinian-made 40-millimeter.

Rockets

Faji-5 Rocket, Iranian-made 122-millimeter.

Qassam Rocket, Palestinian-made 11.5 centimeter.

Drones

Predator Drone, U.S.-made.

Bombs

Dirty Bomb, various terrorists-made.

Pen bomb, Palestinian-made.

Glossary

Abaya: Head-to-toe female Muslim veil (Arab.)

Adonai: My Lord (Heb.)

AEHF: U.S. Air Force Advanced Extremely High Frequency Satellite communications system

Allah o Akbar: God is Great (Arab.)

ASAP: As soon as possible

As salam' alakoom: Peace be upon you; hello (Arab.)

Baklawa: Palestinian dessert; *baklava* (Arab.)

Blimey: Exclamation of surprise (Br.)

Bon: Good (Fr.)

Bon ami: Good friend (Fr.)

Bonjour, comment ca va?:Good day (morning, afternoon); how are you? (Fr.)

C'est la guerre: Such is war (Fr.)

Cheeky: Impertinent (Br.)

CIA: American Counter Intelligence Agency

CIS: Cyprus Intelligence Service

Ciao: So long; goodbye (Italian)

CT²WS: Cognitive Technology Threat Warning System; brainwave binoculars

Djellaba: Desert robe (Arab.)

DGSE: French Directorate General for External Security

EEG binoculars: Brainwave binoculars

ETA: Estimated time of arrival

Fedayeen: Commandos (Arab.)

Flaounes: Stuffed pastries (Cyp.)

Glykos: Fruit and nut sweet dish (Cyp.)

GPS: Global Positioning System

Greek NIS: Greek National Intelligence Service

Guv: Person in a management position (Br.)

Hamas: Iran supported Palestinian terrorist group in control of the Gaza Strip

Holishkies: Jewish stuffed cabbage (Heb.)

Hora: Israeli folk dance (Heb.)

HQ: Headquarters

Hummus: Cooked and mashed chickpeas (Arab.)

ID: Identification

IDF: Israeli Defense Forces

IED: Improvised explosive device

Intel: Intelligence information

IR: Iranian

Irani: Iranian (Per.)

Jihad: Muslim Holy War (Arab., Per.)

Jihadist: One who believes in a Muslim Holy War (Arab.)

Keffiyeh: Desert headdress popular in Palestine (Arab.)

Kibbutz: Group (Heb.)

Kibbutzniks: Kibbutz residents (Heb.)

Koupepias: Stuffed grape leaves (Cyp.)

Lavi: Lion (Heb.)

Maa salama: Goodbye (Arab.)

Madame: Madame (Fr.)

Mais oui: Why yes (Fr.)

MAV: Micro Aerial Vehicle

Metsada: Mossad's Special Operations Division (Heb.)

Merci: Thank you (Fr.)

MI5: British Security Service

MI6: British Secret Intelligence Service

Mossad: Israeli Institute for Intelligence and Special Operations

Muezzin: Islamic caller of the faithful to prayer (Arab.)

Namez: Islamic prayers five times a day (Arab.)

Pardon moi!: Pardon me! (Fr.)

Pastourma: Spicy meat dish (Cyp.)

PLF: Palestinian Liberation Front terrorist group

PLO: Palestinian Liberation Organization terrorist group

Sabbat: Sabbath (Heb.)

Sabra: Israeli national orange and chocolate cordial

Sacré Bleu: Confounded; darn (Fr.)

SAF: British Special Air Force

Sayeret Matkal: Israeli General Staff Reconnaissance commandos (Heb.)

Semi-halo type jump: Low altitude jump with low altitude parachute opening

Shalom!: Hello!; Goodbye!; Peace!; Health! (Heb.)

Sharia Law: Islamic Law (Arab.)

Shatta: Gazan crab stuffed with hot chili peppers (Arab.)

Shekel: Israeli currency (3.5 shekels = $1.00 U.S.)

Sheol: Hades (Heb.)

Shin Bet: Israeli Internal Intelligence Agency

Souk: Bazaar; market (Arab.)

Surganiot: Deep-fried jelly doughnut (Heb.)

SVR: Russian Foreign Intelligence Service

Tactical reload: Reloading a weapon during a firefight and retaining ejected   magazine that may still contain needed ammunition

Takavar: Iranian special forces

Taverna: Tavern (Gr.)

The Prussian: Mossad Director

Tout de suite: At once; immediately (Fr.)

VEVAK: Iranian Secret Police

Wadi: Dry river bed (Arab.)

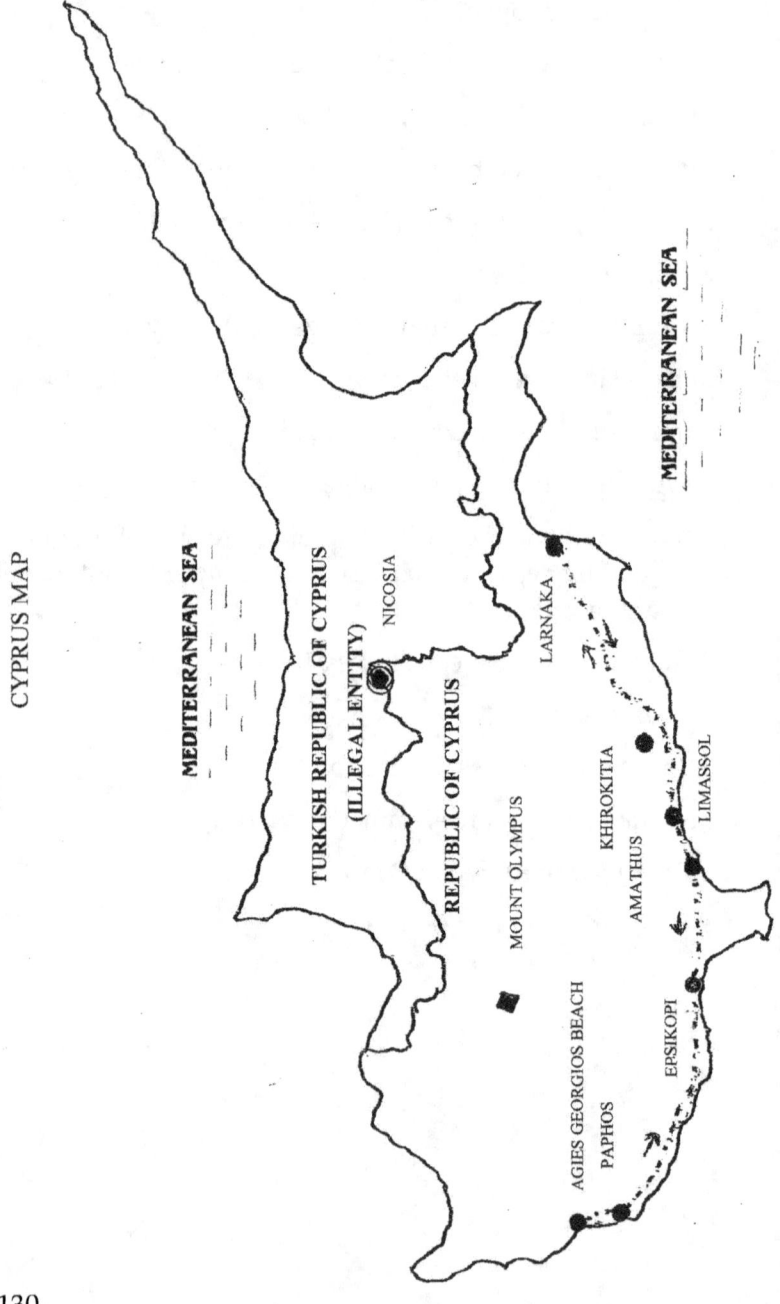

CYPRUS MAP

GAZA STRIP MAP

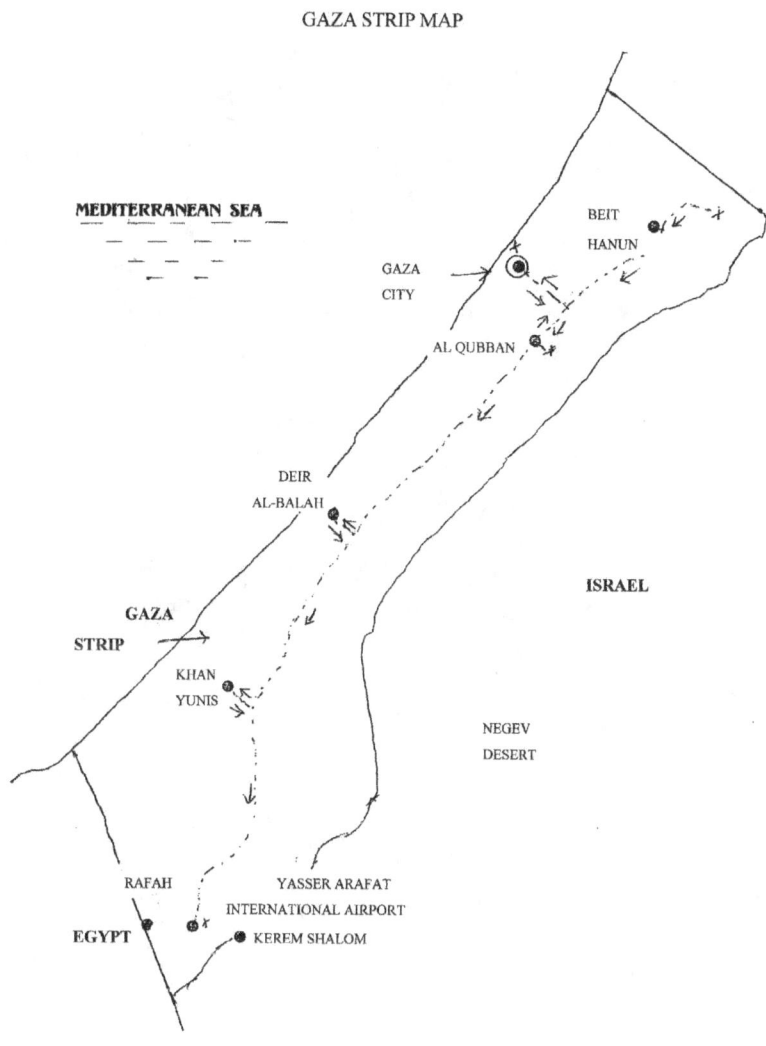

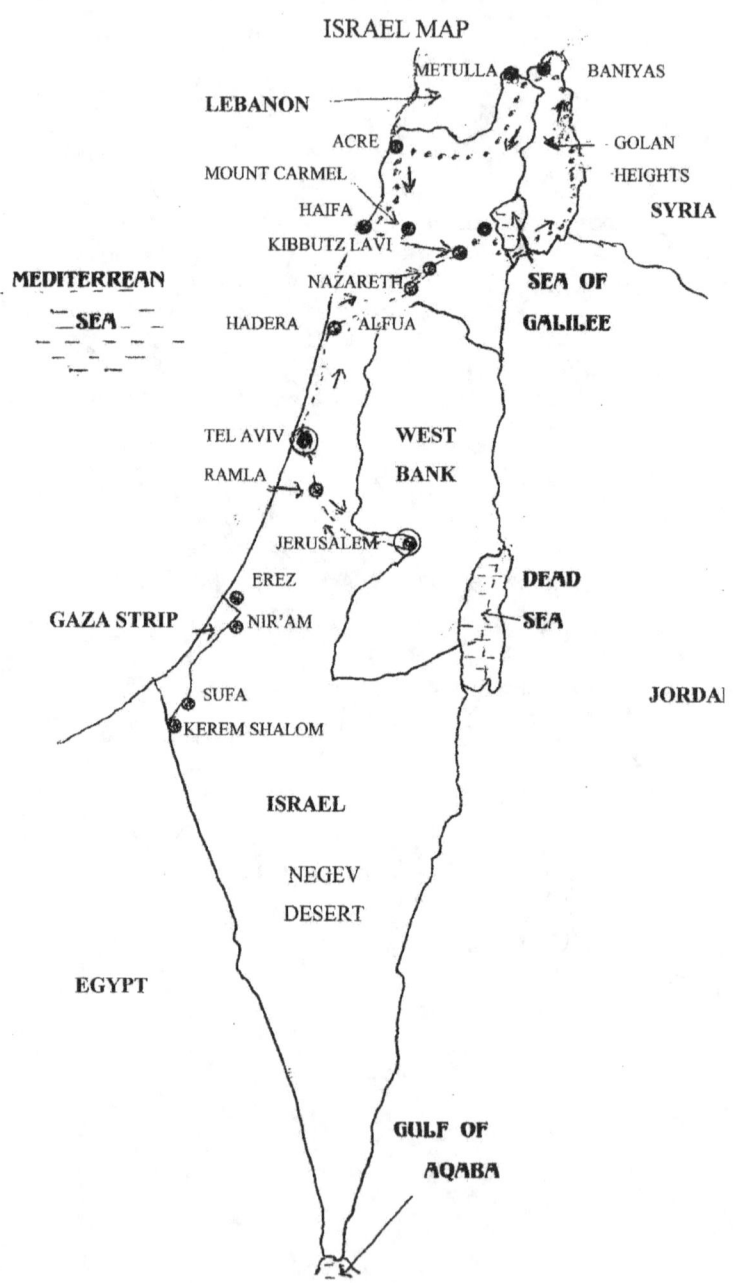

ISRAEL MAP

WEST BANK MAP

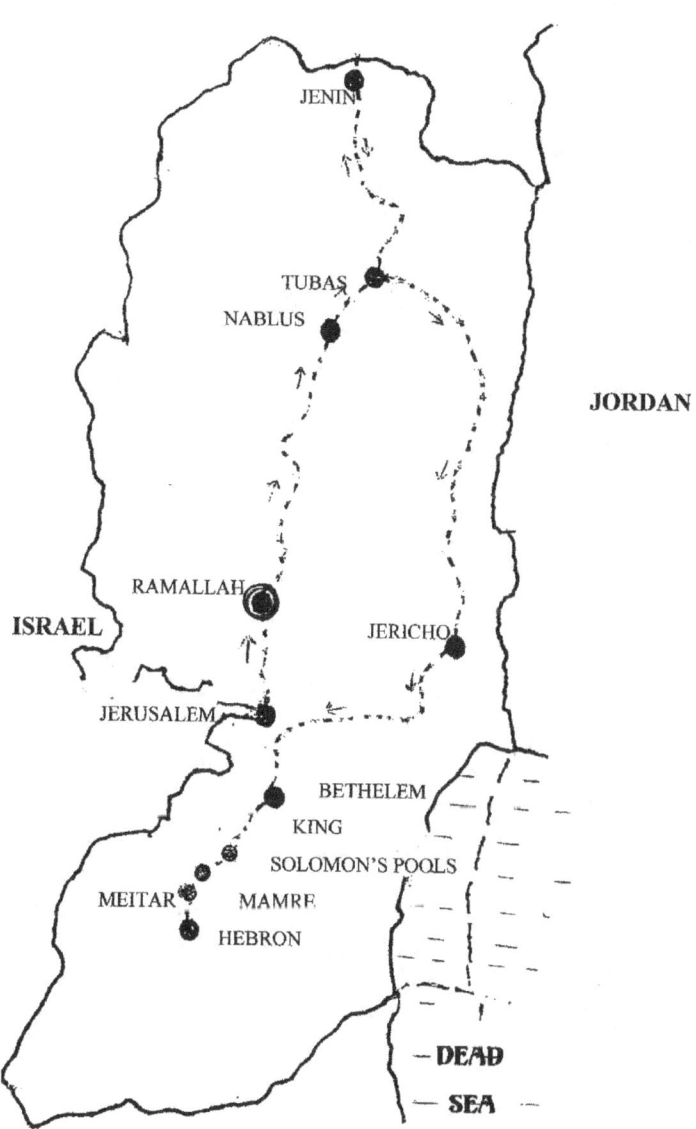